The Great Bamboozlement

The Great Bamboozlement

JANE FLORY

Houghton Mifflin Company   Boston   1982

Library of Congress Cataloging in Publication Data
Flory, Jane, 1917–
The great bamboozlement.

Summary: The Dowells trade their Pennsylvania farm for a Floating Emporium and set off
down the Monongahela River in search of a new
home.
[1. River life—Fiction.   2. Frontier and
pioneer life—Fiction.   3. Boats and Boating—
Fiction]   I. Title.
PZ7.F665Gr   [Fic]   81-17862
ISBN 0-395-31859-9   AACR2

Printed in the United States of America
V 10 9 8 7 6 5 4 3 2 1

Contents

The Great Bamboozlement

1

Mr. Jebbel Hawkins

SERENA COULD HEAR Pa and her brothers singing as they crossed the meadow.

"Can't I go to meet them, Ma?"

Ma was crouched by the hearth, trying to get the fire going. She brushed a strand of hair out of her face and sighed.

"Might as well. You've been housebound all day, and there's no way we can get supper on the table until I get this dadburned fire goin' again."

"I'm sorry about the fire, Ma. It just went out when I wasn't looking."

"It's not your fault, child. The way the chimney leans, you've got to keep an eye on the blaze every minute or the least draft'll blow it out. Go on out, a little fresh air'll do you good."

Serena bounded for the door.

"Take Sweet Harmony along. Keep a tight holt on her. She's rarin' to go for the river."

Sweet Harmony was almost too quick for her, but Serena caught at her sister's dress just in time.

"Let the door stand open," Ma called after her. "Let some of this confounded smoke out."

Serena let her two-year-old sister drag her along, down the hill past the spring and across the partly cleared field. It was still chilly. The early spring air hadn't warmed up much, but it felt so good to be out running after being cooped up in the cramped, smoky cabin.

Ma had worked all day in the field, spading and hoeing. She was determined to get her garden started as soon as the ground was warm enough. Pa and the boys had gone to the woods to chop fence posts. The garden had to be fenced. The deer had to be kept out and Sweet Harmony had to be kept in. Until a yard was built for her, Serena had to stay inside, doing all the house chores and keeping Harmony out of mischief. It had been a long, bothersome day.

Pa and Luke and Newtie were singing at the tops of their lungs, and Newtie was waving a string of fish in time to their music.

"Look!" Newtie hollered as he caught sight of the girls. "Four big ones, and I caught two of them!"

Drat! Confuse and confound! They'd gone fishing without her again. They started out to chop fence posts and ended up at the riverbank. And all day long she'd been stuck inside scrubbing and cleaning and grinding cornmeal and keeping Harmony out of trouble. It wasn't fair. Drat all brothers!

Harmony broke away and ran to Pa, who caught her and tossed her up on his shoulder.

"How's our little lamb?" he asked. "How's our little treasure?"

Serena snorted. "Our little treasure's got us almost worn out. There isn't anything bad she could do that she hasn't tried today. Not one blamed thing."

Pa laughed and began to sing again. After a moment Serena joined in. There wasn't much use in being mad at Pa, or Sweet Harmony either. Didn't get you anywhere.

Ma was still struggling with the fire when they trailed in.

"I can't get the chimney to draw when the wind is in the east," she said.

"It won't draw when the wind's in the north or south either," said Pa. "I guess I'm not much of a chimney builder, Lucinda."

She rose from her knees and stretched her cramped legs.

"No," she said honestly. "No, you're not, and that's the pure truth of it. But then," she added, "there're a lot of other things you are good at, so it evens out."

"Tell me, what other things?" Pa wanted to know.

"Right at this moment I'd be hard pressed to say. But I reckon there must be something. Well, now." She brightened at the sight of the fish. "That's a nice surprise! Luke, take over here and see what you can do to get this fire goin'. Fish for supper! Well, now!"

She started right in to clean the fish. "What'd go nice with these? Fiddleheads, that's what. Serena, you and Newtie see if you can find us enough for supper. Oh, that'd be a pleasure. But don't go far into the woods, now. Dark'll be coming on soon."

"I hope we find a lot," said Newtie as they scratched around in the leaves. "I don't ever want to taste salt beef again. Nor dried squash, neither."

It had been a long winter for the Dowell family. They had moved to the new farm in the early spring of last year, but by the time the cabin had been built and one field partly cleared and planted, summer had been well on its way. The garden was late and skimpy. Only the corn and squash had done at all well. Their small supply of potatoes had soon given out. Serena still remembered the day Pa and Luke rode their old horse way back over the mountains to the nearest settlement and traded him for a whole side of salt beef that they hauled home on their backs.

Pa had been cheerful about it all. "There wasn't much work left in old Geezer," he said, "and we'll need the food long before we'll need him to plow with. You'll see, Lucinda, by the time we're ready for a horse we'll be able to get us a fine team."

Ma had tried to smile, but Serena had been able to see that her heart wasn't in it. "I only hope you're right, Henry. Dear gracious, I hope you're right."

Now Newtie uncovered a nice clump of fiddlehead ferns. The fronds hadn't unfolded yet, and the fiddleheads would cook up tender and sweet.

"Remember the fiddleheads in Green Valley, Serena?"

She did. She remembered the farm in Green Valley well, and the one before that too, although she had been only eight when they had lived there. That was a good place. They had been near a nice little settlement. There had been neighbors and visiting and fun. They hadn't had a neighbor in the three years since.

But Pa said the land was so poor it took two birds to holler one Bob White, so he had traded for the place in Green Valley. The land there was good, but that farm had been too small to support a family. So Pa had traded it for this great big piece of land out here in western Pennsylvania. Acres and acres and acres. But it was all in trees and hills, trees as far as you could see in any direction. Only a small piece of meadowland was open and level, down near the river.

Through the trees Serena could see the Monongahela sparkling way below them. Pa was right. It was a beautiful place. Someday they'd get it cleared and build a better house, and they'd have a real farm. In the meantime it was salt beef and hardscrabble for the Dowells.

"We're all of us well and strong," Pa always said. "I didn't figure on quite so many trees, but we'll manage. As long as there's laughin' and singin' in us we'll make out fine." Pa set great store by laughing and singing.

*

By the time Serena and Newtie got back with the basket of fiddleheads Luke had the fire going fine and bright. Ma was starting to fry the fish and a batch of cornbread was baking on the hearth. Ma was tired to her bones, Serena knew, so she hurried to set the table while Newtie went for more firewood.

While they were all busy at one thing or another, no one thought to keep an eye on Harmony. One minute she was sitting there talking gibberish to her old corn-husk doll, and the next minute she had climbed on a stump stool and was reaching for Ma's mending basket.

"Me sew!" she said as she tipped the basket onto the floor.

"Get her out of there!" Ma cried. "Don't let her lose my thimble!"

Serena scrambled and Sweet Harmony yelled.

"Put it up out of Harm's way." Pa laughed. He bounced the little girl on his knee until her angry sobs turned to giggles. Pa could jolly anyone out of a temper.

Ma sighed. "She's wankly because she's so tired of being shut up inside. But if I let her out she runs straight for the river. Did you get the posts cut to fence in a yard?"

"Well, no," Pa admitted. "We made a good start, but then the axhead flew right off the handle. Have to make a tighter fit. We'll get the rest of those dagnabbed posts out tomorrow for sure."

"I'll fix the ax after supper," Luke offered. Luke was better at fixing things than Pa was, even though he was only thirteen. Pa had wonderful ideas but he wasn't too handy. "We'll get your posts cut tomorrow, Ma," said Luke.

"If you don't stop to go fishing," Serena said to him. She was still smarting at being left out.

"You don't think we went fishin' for pleasure, do you, child?" Pa asked. "Do *you*, Lucinda?"

Ma didn't answer at first. Her lips tightened to a thin line. Then she said, "I don't imagine you disliked it, Henry."

Serena shivered. She hated it when Ma was so bone weary and worried that all the laughing went out of her, when she spoke sharply to Pa. He got that hurt look on his face as if he knew he was to blame but didn't quite know what to do about it.

"Lucinda, we fished for the table! After the ax broke and we couldn't chop anymore, it came to my mind how tired you are of salt beef, and how your eyes'd light up at the sight of a mess of fine catfish. Now, you have to admit they did light up, don't you? And those fish do make mighty fine eatin', don't they?"

Ma probably would have smiled anyway, after a while. She couldn't hold out long when Pa used that teasing, coaxing voice. But the subject was forgotten at a distant sound. It seemed to come up from the river.

"Hark! What's that?"

They all listened as the sound came again.

"A horn of some kind. Someone's coming."

Ma's eyes went to the rifle hanging over the door.

Pa said quickly, "No need to fear, Lucinda. Bad folks don't announce their comin'. Open the door, Luke, and light 'em up the hill. Whoever it is, he'll be a friend."

"You're too trustin', Henry. Harmony, Serena, you stay right here by me."

Pa and the boys were already out the door and starting down the hill.

"It might be another preacher, Ma," Serena said. Last fall a traveling preacher had stopped by. They had had a Sunday service right there in the cabin, even though it had been Tuesday. The preacher said he didn't know when he'd heard such singing, and Pa played the hymns on his mouth organ. "Wouldn't it be nice if it was a preacher?"

Ma didn't answer, but her arm tightened around Serena and she hauled Sweet Harmony up on her lap.

The stranger wasn't a preacher. He was a big, bearded man whose bulk seemed to fill the little cabin. He shook hands all around and said, "Jebbel Hawkins, sir and ma'am. Jebbel Hawkins, peddler. Saw your light through the trees."

Pa and the boys helped him unbuckle the pack and lift it from his shoulders.

"Easy there," he said. "All of the riches of Araby are there, and then some."

He had twinkly eyes and a broad smile, and Ma seemed to relax a little. She hurried to heat up some supper.

"Did you come all this way on foot?" Pa asked. "The path through the woods is rougher'n a hog's back."

"Only up from the riverbank," explained Mr. Hawkins. "The rest of my goods is on a raft, tied up at the foot of your hill. The Hawkins Floating Emporium. Beats pack-peddling any day. I just sit there and let the river do all the work."

Pa nodded. "If only the river would chop trees for me, I'd be perishin' pleased. We've got years of choppin' ahead of us."

While Ma was toasting leftover cornbread, Pa lined up his children and introduced them. Serena looked along the line as Pa said their names. Luke was tall for his age and skinny. His hair was fair and curly like Pa's, and his eyes were blue and gentle. Newtie was a lot shorter. He hadn't gotten his growth yet, being only twelve, but he was stocky and strong. Sweet Harmony had curls too, like the boys, and her eyes were as blue as highbush huckleberries. Only Serena looked like Ma, with straight brown hair and brown eyes.

"Luke, Newton," said Pa. "And Serena, who doesn't always fit her name. Maybe we should have called her Pepperpot."

"Or Tag-along," said Newtie out of the corner of his mouth.

She gave him a jab with her elbow that shut him up in a hurry.

"And here's Sweet Harmony, our littlest. I guess we should have called her Cow's Tail, for she came on be-hind."

Harmony was afraid of the big, bearded stranger. She fled to the safety of Ma's skirt and howled.

"Well," said Pa, laughing and picking her up. "She does beat all. Sometimes Harmony's sweet and sometimes she hollers until my head rings like a kettle. We're hopin' as she ages she'll mellow and live up to her name more. Nothin' on earth is as sweet as harmony."

Ma had heated up some soup. When she said she was sorry there wasn't more, that he should have come in time for the fish, Mr. Hawkins said, "There's a gracious plenty, ma'am. And it'll be heaven compared to my cooking. You don't know how tired I am of my own food. If it isn't burnt, it's underdone. Can't seem to get the hang of it. Oh, this is fine, ma'am."

He must have meant it, for he had three helpings. Lucky the supply of cornmeal was holding out, Serena thought. It would be a long time before the new crop of corn was planted and grown and ready for grinding.

After supper came the good part. Mr. Hawkins opened his pack and spread out his treasures.

"Only the small things are here," he said. "I leave the bigger goods on the raft."

There was no use thinking they could buy much, but it was exciting to see. Combs and candles, gunflints and ginger, buttons and bridle reins, scissors and spices — there seemed to be no end to the wonderful things Mr. Hawkins displayed.

Ma chose three new needles and a comb, and Pa bought a rasp to sharpen his tools.

"You'll make a poor livin' if you have to depend on the likes of us," Pa said.

"Business along the river is pretty good. People have settled in, and they need things, need 'em bad. They hear my horn and see my red flag waving, and they're waiting at the riverbank. Just a question of getting them in the idea of buying and trading. Oh, I'll make me a living, never fear. But it's not what I'd choose to do for long. I'm on the move day after day, never see the same folks two days in a row, never put down roots. I'd trade it all in a minute for a good farm and a fine family like yours, Dowell."

"The farm, maybe, but I can't trade the family." Pa chuckled. "I'd surely hate to part with my family. They're my treasures, even howlin' Harmony."

The baby had fallen asleep on his shoulder. He handed her gently to Ma, and Ma put on her little nightshirt and tucked her into the box beside the bed.

Pa and Mr. Hawkins talked until late, until the fire was no more than a dim glow. Mr. Hawkins had a string of funny stories to tell about his adventures as a peddler. Pa really enjoyed that.

"It certainly is an exciting life," Pa said after they had stopped laughing over one of the escapades. "Life here on the farm tends to get a bit dull." He sighed.

Then Mr. Hawkins told about hundreds of families on the move on rafts and flatboats, and about the rich open land along the Ohio, waiting to be settled.

"I thought eighteen twenty-two was a big year for folks on the go, but this year's going to be bigger. The opportunities lie further west, no doubt about it."

Serena and the boys listened to it all, first wide-eyed and then sleepy-eyed and finally yawning and struggling to keep awake. Pa invited Mr. Hawkins to spread his blanket on the hearth before the fire, but the genial peddler shook his head.

"The raft rocks me just like a cradle," he said.

"Then stop by for breakfast," Pa urged. "We do enjoy company and a good talk."

Serena and Luke and Newtie stumbled drowsily up the ladder to the loft. The boys fell asleep right away, and Serena was not long behind them.

Pa and Ma weren't talked out, though. Serena could hear their voices, low, urgent, going on and on. They seemed to be arguing about something.

She wondered what it could be, and fell asleep still wondering.

2

A Change of Plans

BREAKFAST THE NEXT morning was a jolly affair. Mr. Hawkins turned up early, and while Serena fed the chickens and Luke and Newtie tended to the cow and the pigs, Pa showed Mr. Hawkins the farm. He pointed out where the new big barn would stand, and where the fields of grain would grow once the land was cleared.

"This slope'll be grand for an orchard," said Mr. Hawkins. "Full sunlight, and it'll be sheltered from frosts."

"Apples," said Pa. "And cherries'll do well, and maybe even peaches and apricots someday. Oh, we'll have a fine fruit crop here."

Serena tagged along behind them. They didn't seem to see the brush and brambles and the dense shade of tall trees. They saw cleared land rolling away on all sides, and the fruit hanging heavy on the young apple trees.

"Oh, I do envy you, Dowell. This spot will be a garden of Eden. You have only to set plow to it to make it produce mightily."

"Well, yes," said Pa. "Plowin', that's the rub. The trees have to be cut and the stumps dragged out first." He seemed to come down to earth with a thud.

"Time," said Mr. Hawkins, who was still dreaming of the future. "Time is all it takes, and a mite o' sweat. I wish it were mine, I do indeed. There's a young lady back home who has given me her promise to wed, but not until I've a roof over my head and a table to put my feet under. Well, maybe by next year — "

"Hmmm," said Pa. "Hmmm."

Ma had the cornmeal mush ready by the time they climbed back up to the cabin, and again Mr. Hawkins ate as if he enjoyed every mouthful. Between bites he told them how lucky they were.

At last he pushed back his plate. He said he had to leave, though he didn't feel ready. They said good-by and urged him to come by on his way back. Luke and Newtie had started out the door with him when Pa turned back and said something to Ma in an urgent whisper.

"No!" Ma answered. "I haven't changed my mind. Here we are and here we stay!"

"I can at least ask, Lucinda. No harm in just askin', is there?"

"You won't stop there, once you get an idea in your head."

Ma was beginning to cry, and she groped for a corner of her apron as Pa said, "If it's a good idea, Lucinda, if it's a step up?"

"They've all seemed like good ideas, Henry, and here we are years later and not settled in yet."

"Open level land, you heard him tell about it. Rich and open and ready to farm. We'd get in a real crop this very year. And we'd have an adventure in the meantime, don't you see?"

"That's it!" Ma yelled through her tears. "That's it! The adventure of it is what strikes you, that and ridin' down the river, with the river doin' all the work. Well, ask then, and the devil take you if he says yes, for I'll have no part of it!"

She flung her apron over her head and slumped on a stool, crying as if her heart would break.

"Lucinda, you'll come to see what a good move it is. Lucinda, honey — "

Ma did not answer, and Pa slammed out of the cabin and ran down the hill after Mr. Hawkins and the boys.

Serena stood there, stunned. This was dreadful. Never in all their disagreements had Ma and Pa ever come to anything like this. Serena didn't know what to do. After a while she cleared away the breakfast things. Ma was still hiccupping away, so she dipped out a mug of water and tried to get Ma to drink it. She patted her mother's back, and felt how thin and bony it was under the homespun cloth.

"Now, now," she said, using the same words Ma did in comforting her children. "There now, it'll be all right. Things'll work out fine." Serena wished she was as sure as she sounded.

Finally Ma dried her eyes. She stood up and said in a shaky voice, "What's done is done and can't be helped. Let's at least see how it's comin' out."

Together they stood in the doorway and looked down the hill. They could see Pa and Mr. Hawkins down in the meadow, talking a mile a minute. Luke and Newtie weren't talking, but they certainly were listening. Serena felt the familiar stab of envy. Wouldn't you know they'd be right in the thick of whatever was going on, and she was still wondering. She wanted to ask Ma what it was all about, but maybe that would start the tears again.

Suddenly Pa and Mr. Hawkins clapped each other on the back and shook hands. With a whoop Pa started up the path to the cabin. Ma sagged against the door frame.

"I was hopin' and prayin' against him," she said, "but it didn't do any good. He's gone and done it."

Pa reached the top of the hill.

"Lucinda! Lucinda, honey, he said yes! We made the deal!"

He grabbed Ma's hands and swung her around. Like it or not, she had to join in his joyful dance.

"We made the deal, Lucinda! I traded him the farm!"

*

There was a lot to do in a few short days. First Pa and Mr. Hawkins sat down together and listed everything that was to be traded: the land and the cabin — but not the livestock; Pa knew Ma wouldn't stand for that — in exchange for the raft and almost everything in the Floating Emporium. Mr. Hawkins reserved only a few tools that he'd need to get started.

At first Ma stayed out of the discussion, refusing to have anything at all to do with the trade. But Serena could see that she was softening as she heard Mr. Hawkins say, "Seventeen full bolts of calico, all colors."

"All colors! Well, now," said Ma to herself.

"And plenty of ribbons — never does to run out of ribbons. Sometimes it pays to throw in enough ribbon for a hair bow if you've made a good sale. Or a few nice buttons, or some such pretties. Makes the customer happy to see you next time around."

"There won't be a next time around," Ma reminded Pa sharply. "You promised this is only until we find our new farm."

"Only until then, Lucinda. I promise."

The boys were delighted with the trade, but Serena was of two minds about it. Of course it was going to be exciting, drifting down the Monongahela into the Ohio River, having who knew what kinds of adventures, doing whatever it was boat-storekeepers did. But it had all happened so suddenly. One day they were settled on their hilly farmland, making plans for years to come. The next minute they were homeless, landless wanderers. It didn't seem real.

Not until the papers were drawn up and signed did she believe it. Up until that moment she kept thinking that something would surely happen, that Pa would suddenly laugh and say it was all one of his jokes.

Perhaps Ma thought so too. But when Mr. Hawkins stood up from the table with the deed to the farm in his hand, and when Pa said, "Well, Lucinda, it's done. The Floating Emporium is all ours," only then did Ma really take it all in. There were no tears then, only a wry smile as Pa hugged her.

"There's no turnin' back now," she said. "Now the work begins."

First the raft. What was plenty big enough for one was not nearly roomy enough for six. Ma said she wouldn't put up with the shaky little lean-to that Mr. Hawkins had been bunking in. A real cabin, she insisted. And a place for the animals.

"They're the start of our new farm," she said firmly. "The critters are to be housed proper."

"Lucinda, if you insist on all that, we'll be pokin' around here all summer, just gettin' ready to leave."

"It'll save time in the long run," Ma said. "We've got the trees right here, if Mr. Hawkins will give us leave to chop a few. We can build a small shanty and move it right onto our new farm soon as we find it."

Mr. Hawkins said they could have all the trees they needed and welcome, and he even offered to stay on for a few days and help them. Later he would try to get a ride on some flatboat poling upriver and bring back his new wife.

So they set to work cutting trees. The two men and Luke chopped them down, and Ma and Serena and Newtie sawed off the limbs and hacked away at the branches.

At first they didn't know what to do with Sweet Harmony. Serena had a feeling she would be delegated to watch the little girl, so she said quickly, "Why can't we tie her to a tree down by the riverbank? She can see everything that's going on, but she won't be able to fall in."

Harmony had her cornhusk doll to play with, and Mr. Hawkins found her a cowbell to ring. All day long she clanged and hollered, as happy, Pa said, as a bear in a bee tree.

They made the raft three times as big as it had been, and built a cabin large enough to sleep six.

"We're going to be rivermen!" protested Newtie. "Ring-tailed roarers! We don't want to sleep inside."

"You will, come a pour-down," said Ma. "We'll have a roof."

There was no time for cutting and drying shingles and no straw for a proper thatch, so they did the best they could with leafy branches, woven in and out of thin willow whips.

"Not very neat," said Ma. She stood on the bank directing while Serena and Newtie scrambled over the roof, tucking in branches where it seemed thin. "Not neat at all, truth to tell, but it'll do. It'll shed the rain, and we'll have to settle for that."

"We can lash Lilybelle's dried grass to the roof," sug-

gested Serena. "It'll help keep out the rain, and we can pitch it down as she needs it."

"Why can't we put the chicken coop up here?" Newtie called down. "Plenty of room for the chickens to move around, and we can toss their feed up."

There were branches to spare, so Serena added a leafy fence around the flat roof, enough to keep the hens in. It was a funny-looking cabin, but finally Ma said it would do.

"For the short time we'll be needin' it," she added, to make sure Pa understood that this move was only temporary.

Fixing up the raft was hard work. Each evening they had just enough strength to drag up to the cabin on the hill for supper. They started before dawn and worked as long as there was light to see, with only a short time to eat and rest at noon when the sun stood overhead.

Pa had a good idea for the store, and Mr. Hawkins and Luke built it. They cut a window into the side wall of the store, with a hinged flap to cover it. The flap came down to make a counter and it let light and air inside. At night it could be closed up tight to keep out the damp river air.

"You've got a knack for storekeeping," said Mr. Hawkins. "You take to it like you were born in a store."

Ma looked uneasy. Then she smiled a little as she looked at the crowded shelves. "Gives me the wonderment to see all this," she said. "Don't seem real to me."

At last everything was ready. Ma had decided they'd sleep one last night in the cabin and leave early the next morning. Luke and Newtie and Serena wanted to move onto the raft right away. Finally, because she saw they'd never get to sleep at all if she didn't say yes, Ma said it.

"I give up beat. Fetch your haybags and make up your beds, then, and be off with you. The rest of us'll follow come morning."

The raft rocked gently. Serena lay on her haybag looking up at the stars that clustered close overhead.

"So near," she murmured. "I bet I could reach out and grab me a handful."

It had been a long hard day, and she was asleep before she could get her handful of glitter.

3

The Dowells Afloat

BY THE TIME the sun was up the next morning the hens were scratching around on the roof of wilted leaves as if they had always lived there. The cow and the pigs were led onto the raft, mooing and squealing. There was some loud complaining from the pigs about the ground that shifted and dipped under them, but they soon settled down.

Mr. Hawkins untied the ropes. For a moment nothing happened, and then the raft swung out into the current. Pa heaved on the sweep oar as Mr. Hawkins had instructed, and they were on their way.

"Good-by, good luck!" they shouted to Mr. Hawkins. He stood on the bank, waving.

"I plumb forgot to point out that the cabin leans and the chimney doesn't draw," Pa remembered.

"He'll find out," said Ma. "That's one of the first things his new wife'll notice."

In a few minutes they were out of sight of Mr. Hawkins. The cabin on the hill was his now. It was only a memory for the Dowells. Ma wiped her eyes on her apron, and that was that. They were on their way.

The raft didn't ride so smoothly at first. Pa was working too hard at steering. First he'd swing too far toward the right bank, and just before they'd hit it he'd strain at the sweep oar and pull them out again, this time too far to the left.

Luke and Newtie were hollering, "Look out, Pa! Watch out! Left, left! No, right!"

But after a while Pa got the hang of it.

"Just have to trust the river more," he said. "The current knows where to take us if I don't thrash around and fight it."

He learned to lean on the sweep and let the river do the work. After that the raft glided easily between the high wooded banks on either side. It hardly seemed to be moving at all, yet Serena could see the trees passing swiftly.

"We're on our way, Ma," she said. "At this rate we'll be down the Monongahela before we know it. We'll find our new farm, and plant the garden, and — "

Ma nodded, but she did not smile.

"We aren't there yet," she said.

While they had been chopping and hauling logs, Mr. Hawkins had told Pa all he could about navigating on the river. He had warned about hidden rocks and fallen trees. He had told Pa how to steer around a bend, and how to tie a knot that would hold fast when they tied up. He had smoothed off a piece of earth and on it scratched a map of the Monongahela's twists and turns.

"Goes back and forth," he had said, "crooked as a snake's trail, but down to here it's fairly calm. Then about here, between this bend and that, there's a run of rapids — not dangerous, mind, but tricky. And after that the hills flatten out some on either side and the river runs deeper. Easier to navigate."

"Hmmm," Pa had said, studying the diagram.

"Now do tie up at night, no matter how much of a hurry you're in. You can always find some sort of little bay where you can pull in out of the current. You won't likely meet more'n a handful of boats between here and maybe Brownsville. Traffic's thin where the river is shallow. Maybe a couple of settlers' rafts, and some flatboats certainly. And mind this, be careful when you come across a riverman, one of those fellows on a flatboat. Don't know why, but they pride themselves on being poison mean. Don't rile 'em up if you can help it. They don't call themselves ring-tailed roarers for nothing."

The Dowells had listened and nodded soberly. But as they rode along that first bright day they found nothing to be sober about. The sun was warm; the sky was blue. The red trading flag flapped lazily from the flagpole. Pa sang at the sweep, and Luke and Newtie and Serena whistled as they baited their hooks for catfish. At least here on the river the boys had to include her when they went fishing, like it or not. They couldn't get away from her.

Sweet Harmony puttered around at the end of a tether. She explored everywhere, peering in at the cow and the pigs. Finally she settled down on the sunny side of the shanty, happily banging on a pan with a wooden spoon.

Ma felt at loose ends. Dinner was a long time off, and until then there was just nothing she had to do. She wandered restlessly about at first, and then she settled in the sunshine to knit. After a while she began to hum to Pa's tune.

"This is the life," said Pa. He had turned the sweep over to Luke and was stretched out by Ma's side. "Plenty of time for singin' and laughin', and the river does all the work. Just for now," he added hastily, with a look at Ma. "Just for a time until we find our new farm."

Ma seemed to breathe easier at that. She smiled at Pa. "It is right pleasant," she admitted.

Newtie was the one who first saw the clearing.

"Pa!" he shouted. "There's a settlement ahead! Steer us in to shore, Luke!"

Luke pulled too hard on the oar and the raft swung around with a lurch. Pa sprang to his feet, yelling, "Hold it! Hang on, Luke, hold her steady."

It took both of them to get the clumsy raft on a straight course again, headed in toward shore.

Serena tooted on the boat horn to give notice of their coming. By the time Pa had urged the raft to shore and tied it securely to a tree stump, five or six people had gathered at the landing.

"There's the red flag! It's the Hawkins Floating Emporium!"

Not anymore, thought Serena. It belongs to the Dowells now. We'll have to change that sign on the side of the store.

"Now, keep in mind," said Pa, "this is serious business. We must act dignified. We're about to make our first sale."

They were as still as mice, even Sweet Harmony.

Pa cleared his throat. He cleared it again. Then he said in a low voice, "Well, anyone interested in buyin' can step forward onto the raft."

There was a shuffling of feet, but no one made a move toward the raft.

"Well," said Pa again. "Well —"

Someone tittered. Pa's face turned as red as a flannel petticoat. He tried again.

"We've got a fine mess of goods inside . . ."

Serena felt just terrible. Was nobody going to buy anything?

Finally one man said, "I might could use a hoe."

"Certainly, sir," said Pa, very serious and dignified. He turned to find a hoe, but in the clutter of the shanty he couldn't locate one.

"Here's a good rake," he said hopefully. "And here's a shovel —"

"They ain't quite the same thing, storekeeper," said

the customer, and the onlookers laughed a little.

"Smart alecks," whispered Ma fiercely.

"I'm short of cornmeal," a woman said after a time. Pa found that, and filled her wooden container.

"That'll be — that'll come to — that's about ten pennies' worth."

"That's about four pennies more'n I plan to give," she answered. "Six is aplenty by my count."

Pa took the six pennies meekly. No one seemed to want to step on board the Floating Emporium to look over the goods, so after a pause Pa said, "Well, folks, it's been nice to make your acquaintance. We'd best be gettin' on. Shove off, boys."

They rode for a long time without talking. Then Pa said, "Six pennies. Only six miserable pennies. I guess I'm no good at storekeepin'."

His voice was so sad it almost broke Serena's heart. Ma's too, for she said quickly, "Now Henry, you're not to feel dismal. You'll figure out how it's done. You're a pure wonderment at figurin' out the knack of things. You'll do it. You can bamboozle 'em, you know you can. Next time things'll be better."

Pa brightened. "Bamboozlement, that's the ticket. But how? What kind of bamboozlement, Lucinda?"

"You'll figure it out, Henry. You'll see, next time'll be much better."

Pa leaned on the sweep, deep in thought, and no one disturbed him.

Serena watched him. "Ma," she whispered. "Bamboozling — isn't that deceitful? Isn't it trickery? Pa won't cheat folks, will he? Lie to 'em?"

Ma said indignantly, "Not your pa. Not Henry. When he says bamboozle he means jokin' and coaxin' and turnin' folks around to his way of thinkin' in a laughin' sort of way. You don't ever need to worry about your pa's kind of bamboozlement, Serena. You wait and see."

It was a little better next time. A little, but not much. By the time they tied up to eat, Pa had taken in sixteen more pennies, and they had gotten rid of three yards of yellow calico and some buttons.

"You'll get the knack of it," Ma insisted. "You'll do it. Don't give up."

"I daren't," Pa said mournfully. "I got to keep tryin', no matter what. I traded our farm for this, Lucinda. This store is all we've got."

They ate their supper in silence. There just didn't seem to be much to say.

Pa did a lot of thinking during the night. After breakfast the next morning he said, "They won't catch me out twice. Afore we stop again I'll know every piece in the shanty. Where it is and how much it costs. Take the sweep, Luke. I got me some studyin' to do."

And he did. He took everything off the shelves, off the nails on the shanty walls, and from the hooks on the ceiling, one by one. He opened barrels and boxes and finally he was satisfied that he knew where everything was kept. His spirits began to rise again.

"There's more to storekeepin' than I dreamed, Lucinda. I may not have it quite by the tail yet, but I'm on my way. At least I won't have to look such a fool, and that's a mercy."

"You never looked like a fool to us, Pa," Serena said loyally. "You'll do just fine. You'll see."

The smile he gave her was only a pale shadow of his usual wide grin, but by the time they had made the next two stops he was whistling a little.

"I'm doin' a mite better," he said. "If they ask for molasses, I don't have to offer vinegar, at any rate."

"Molasses'll do fine on the cornbread for dinner," said Ma. "Cornbread and the poke greens I found when we were tied up, and fish, if you young 'uns have any good fortune."

Serena tugged on her line. She jiggled it up and down, but nothing happened. She had fished all day with nary a nibble, and that was discouraging. Luke had caught two little ones, and Newtie, always the best fisherman, had hauled in three. Luke had figured out another of his inventions, a rigging that let them leave their poles and go about their chores. When a fish bit, the bobbing line pulled on a harness bell and called them back to haul the catch in. It was a fine idea, but the trouble was they had few chores to call them away, and fewer bites.

Serena had none. In all this big river, surely there was one catfish that could take an interest in Serena Dowell's line.

They soon came to a clearing with a dozen or so houses clustered close together. Reluctantly Serena set down her pole. With her luck, she thought, the fish would start biting as soon as she left. She went to get the boat horn. That had come to be her chore, and she blew the horn for all she was worth.

She blew it again, and in a short time a good-sized crowd was gathered on the riverbank. The Dowells all stood quietly as Pa issued his invitation to step aboard the Floating Emporium. Before anyone could take him up on his offer, there was a splash and a tinkle on the far side of the raft.

Serena let out a yelp of surprise and leaped for her fishing line. She completely forgot that storekeeping was a serious and dignified business. She only remembered that she had been fishing all day and this was her first bite.

"It's a whopper!" she shouted. "I caught me a hundred-pound whopper! Luke, help, I can't haul him in alone!"

There was a wild splashing and struggling, and in a moment they had hauled in the biggest catfish Serena had ever seen.

"Big as a whale!" yelled Newtie. "Yippee! Yippee!"

Sweet Harmony crashed her pan and spoon and yelled, "Yippee!"

"By ginger!" said Pa. He too forgot that he was a serious storekeeper. "By dabs! That child do beat all! Enough catfish for a fish fry! How about it, folks, did you ever see a finer catch?"

The folks on the bank allowed as how they never did. Serena said it must be the new fishhooks she was using, and that did it.

First a tall skinny man hopped on the raft, saying he was bound he'd have some of the same hooks. Then a short little woman said if he was about to catch such fish, she'd need cornmeal to fry 'em in, and the rush started.

The folks bought thread and pins and tin cups and nails. One lady said she had a desperate need of tooth–ache remedy, but she hadn't a spare cent. Pa said he'd be interested in trading. He got a bag of seed potatoes and she got her toothache medicine and they both were happy about the deal.

Pa was still the only one who knew where everything was, but all the Dowells sorted through the goods and held up anything that looked interesting.

"Scissors, anybody?" called Luke, and a woman found she needed scissors. "Tobaccy? Pipes? A fine shovel . . . who needs a good hammer? We've aplenty."

Someone even bought Harmony's pan and spoon. She set up a yell until Serena found her cowbell, and then she was contented to go dingdonging through the crowd, tangling folks in her tether.

The buying and selling lasted so long that the Dowells decided to stay tied up right there for the night. Pa counted the money and announced happily, "Three dollars and fifty-three cents, a bag of seed potatoes, a bag of pigeon feathers, a quarter-pound of mustard seed, and three muskrat skins. By ginger, that wasn't a bad day. And we owe it all to Serena's monster catfish."

4

Excitement Ashore

PA HAD DONE some thinking, and the next day he said, "By dabs, I didn't have the sense to pull in my head when I slammed the door! I've been goin' at things all wrong. I can see as clear as well water we need a bit of excitement to start us off. That catfish did it."

Serena was worried. "I'll try, Pa, but I'd be a guaranteed wonder if I could make a catfish bite every time we needed some excitement."

"Well, no, Serena. That'd be too much to expect. But there's more'n one way of gettin' out of a skunk hole, and I aim to try."

"You'll come up with something," said Ma. "You're a guaranteed wonder yourself at comin' up with things.

Now fetch me some cook-wood, somebody, and we'll have breakfast in a hurry."

Pa studied it out, and sure enough, he came up with an idea. "I was tryin' to be somethin' I wasn't ever meant to be. You know as well as I do I'm not serious and dignified, Lucinda. Let's see what happens when we just let ourselves have a little fun."

The next time the Floating Emporium pulled into a landing they did it according to Pa's new plan. Luke took the sweep oar so Pa could play the mouth organ, and they all sang. Serena tooted the boat horn between verses, and Sweet Harmony clanged her cowbell. When enough people gathered, Pa stopped playing and made a speech.

"Step right on board, ladies and gents! You are about to see the finest goods ever peddled on the old Mo-non-ga-hela! The prettiest calicoes, the sharpest tools, the sweetest rock candy. We've even got a jug of the world's slowest-runnin' molasses! Step up, step up, don't miss it!"

This time they did step up. That evening Pa counted the coins that had clinked into the strongbox.

"By ginger, Lucinda, this tradin' is an everlastin' happiness. Never in my life did I enjoy myself so much. But it's only until we find our farm," he added quickly. "I expect we'll find the right spot as soon as we get out of this hilly country."

*

[35]

They settled comfortably into their new way of life. There was a little excitement when they first came to rapids, until Pa got the hang of navigating them. They all grabbed poles then and helped shove the raft through the turbulent water that boiled and eddied around the rocks. It was scary when the raft lurched and slipped and plunged, and their shouts echoed from the high rocky walls on either side of the river.

But that was soon over. Ma said, "No more harm than a few gray hairs, thank goodness," and the river deepened and ran smooth as glass through the deep forests. It was chilly there, where the sun didn't reach. Lonesome and spooky and chilly. Serena was glad of her shawl. Soon, though, they slid into the sunshine, where the river spread out between low flower-covered banks. They drifted along at what Pa figured was about two miles an hour, from settlement to settlement.

Whenever they could, they tied up at night at a spot where they could tether Lilybelle, the cow, on the riverbank to graze. They gathered greens for the chickens and pigs before breakfast and cleaned out the pigpen with buckets of water. Cleaning the pen had never been anything but hard work before, but now they laughed and sloshed water on themselves and the pigs and then sat out in the sun to dry off.

Even Ma unbent and admitted she was enjoying the easy way of doing things.

"I'll be spoiled rotten," she said. "I won't want to lift a hoe again." But she smiled as she said it, and went on with the dress she was making for Serena. It was of pink calico. Ma said, "I'd feel surer if I could see the new fashion, see if it's tucks or gathers. I'll just have to do the best I can."

"Tucks or gathers, don't make no never-mind," said Pa. "Our Serena'll be pretty as a picture in it."

Serena could hardly wait for the dress to be ready, but on the raft there wasn't much to do but wait. There was plenty of pleasant scenery to look at and occasionally some other water travelers. Quite often a huge lumber raft passed them, going faster than they were because six big oarsmen were rowing as fast as they could.

"They sell off the lumber to sawmills along the river," Pa said. "They don't waste a minute gettin' there, do they? Blowin' and honkin' at us like that! All right, all right, we'll move over. There's river enough for both of us."

The Dowells always waved in answer to the shouted greetings and watched a little nervously until the ring-tailed roarers were out of sight.

Once in a while they passed a settler's raft tied up at the river's edge. Ma gave each one a good looking-over.

"They're carrying a pair of mules," she would report, "but they don't seem to have a cow. I wonder where they're heading for? Did you see what a bunch of young 'uns they had? None big enough to be much help with plowin'. Thank goodness for Luke and Newtie."

And for me too, Serena thought. I could be as handy with a plow as Newtie any day, and he knows it.

The boys had begun to accept Serena as an equal. They had to admit she was as patient a fisherman as either of them. She dug her own worms and baited her own hook so they could not say she was a fraidy-cat girl.

When Luke and Newtie took the gun to hunt for rabbits, they let her trail along to carry the game if they shot any. She pestered Pa to let her try to get her own rabbit.

"Wait," he said. "That gun's got a powerful kick, and you're only a sprig yet. Wait a while."

Behind the shanty where no one could see she practiced sighting down the unloaded gun. She got so she could swing it to her shoulder and fire like an experienced marksman. She sighed and then grinned. "At least this way I never miss."

It was hard to wait, but she had no choice. So she put the gun inside the shanty door and went to dip for waterbugs to amuse Sweet Harmony.

They floated downriver, pulling in to tie up at each likely settlement along the riverbank. And at almost every stop Pa's storekeeping went well. He joked with the customers and traded stories as he traded molasses and coonskins.

Ma and the children were quick enough at finding things and remembering prices and making change, but it was Pa who was best at matching wits and bargaining. He had a magic touch, Ma admitted. The toughest trader somehow ended up feeling the winner, while Pa grinned over the good deal he had made.

One of the hens had gone broody, and Pa bargained for a clutch of duck eggs for her to sit on.

"Fancy it!" said Ma, delighted at the prospect. "Ducks! I only hope we find our farm before she hatches them out. We'll have our hands full trying to keep four ducklings out of the water."

Serena made a shady little nest on the roof where the hen could sit on the eggs and feel safe under the overhanging leaves.

"We'll have to change the name to the Floating Farm," she giggled, but at that Ma's smile turned to a frown.

"Never!" she snapped. "Our farm'll be on dry land, good level dry land. We're only floatin' just long enough to find it." Then she relented a little. "I guess there's no harm in enjoyin' the floatin' while it lasts, but only until we find our farm, you understand."

The spring days passed quickly, one after another. They did enjoy the floating, even Ma.

Of all the settlements where the Floating Emporium stopped, none had been bigger than five or six or maybe a dozen cabins clustered together, so they were not prepared for the town of Brownsville. When they rounded the bend in the river and saw Brownsville laid out in front of them, all of them gasped. There were real houses all along the bank — real wooden houses, not log cabins. There were sheds and boat shops and a lumberyard. And all the kinds of flatboats that Brownsville was noted for. It was the biggest town any of them had ever seen.

"We won't do well here," Pa said. "A town this big'll have its own stores, like as not."

"But we'll stop anyway, won't we, Pa?" Luke begged. "Don't let's just go past without stopping."

"Pa! Ma! Look! That must be a steamboat!"

As Serena pointed the raft was caught in the steamboat's wash. It rose on the wave and dipped. Serena and Ma were tipped off their feet. Luke and Newtie tumbled. They could hear a crash in the store as a pile of goods fell over. Sweet Harmony rolled over and over, but her tether held her fast. Only Pa managed to keep his feet, but that was because he was hanging onto the sweep oar.

"We'll have to get used to that from now on. The river is deeper from here on down, deep enough for steamboats. We won't have the Monongahela all to ourselves."

Newtie gazed after the steamboat, wide-eyed. "Look at her go," he marveled. "Smoking and puffing and going like the wind!"

Pa said there wasn't much use to open up the store, but there was no reason that they couldn't tie up long enough to walk around the town and see what was to be seen. "I'll stay here and stow our goods away so things won't be beat around every time a steamboat passes," he said. "Now you all go and have yourselves a mite of enjoyment."

They were ready in minutes. Ma gave the girls' hair a hasty slick with the comb and tied on their sunbonnets.

"Luke, Newtie, come back here!" But the boys were off and running up the riverbank. Serena watched them go, Luke with his long legs well in the lead. Newtie was pegging along behind. They must have heard Ma, but they didn't turn back.

"They look like pure raggle-taggles," complained Ma. She didn't complain much. She was smiling at the prospect of a walk through the town.

They went along slowly. Sweet Harmony was a hard one to walk with. She wanted to stop and examine each shaving from the wood shops, each weed and pebble she saw. When Ma tried to carry her she kicked and thrashed. Finally Ma and Serena each took a hand. By that time they were past the Bunby lumberyard and the Bunby carpentry shop and into the town itself. There was so much to see that even Sweet Harmony behaved herself.

The houses were a pure wonderment: two, sometimes even three stories high, with real glass windows sparkling in the sun. There was a real street running between the houses, the dirt packed so hard it was easy to walk on. There was a church with a bell in the steeple.

And the stores. They couldn't believe the stores. There was a boat supply place, the Bunby Marine Supply, with ropes and lanterns. There was a big impressive bank owned, the sign said, by Matthew Bunby, Esquire. There was an apothecary's shop, and a general store. It seemed to have everything on display.

"Not a thing here we don't have on the Floating Emporium," said Ma loyally, "but don't it look grand all spread out like that? We'll have to tell Pa."

Everywhere they went there were groups of people talking. Storekeepers were out on the sidewalk; housewives stood on their doorsteps calling to their neighbors.

"Reckon that's what it's like in town," said Ma. "Nothin' much to do and all day to gossip."

Serena didn't notice. She had eyes only for the shop windows. A milliner's shop in the front room of a house had a bonnet displayed in the window. Ma drew in her breath.

"It's so beautiful," she said. "I never dreamed bonnets came so beautiful. Prettier'n a June rabbit."

She had a hard time tearing herself away but finally she sighed and said, "No place to wear it if I had it. We should be gettin' back to the raft. Now, if we could just round up the boys . . ."

They found Luke and Newtie on the edge of a noisy group around the town pump. Ma beckoned to them and they left reluctantly.

"There's been a big robbery, and we wanted to hear the rest of it," complained Newtie.

"A robbery? Maybe that explains all the talkin' and standin' around. I couldn't imagine that even townspeople had so much time on their hands. A robbery? That's dreadful, but it's not our concern," said Ma. "Your pa'll be itchin' to move on. With any luck we might make another stop or two before sundown."

"It could concern us if we could find the robbers," said Luke. "There's a reward out for catching the three men who did it. Two tall ones and a short fat feller. They robbed the bank of this Bunby man who owns half of Brownsville. They got all the money from the lumberyard and the stores and the boat building."

Newtie said, "They got most all the money there was in town and carried it away in a valise. They lit out down toward the river. Probably split up and headed downstream. That's what everybody was saying."

"I'd sure like to catch the varmints. I'd tie 'em up and claim the reward," said Luke. "We could get ourselves a horse with the reward money. We could get a team, maybe."

"I'd give 'em a pure talking-to before I put them in jail. I'd teach 'em not to be so lowdown. And then I'd spend the reward on two good rifles, one for each of us," said Newtie.

But none for me, Serena thought bitterly. They never think I'd like to have a rifle too.

Then she brightened. I'll earn the reward money myself and buy my own rifle, and I'll get the blue silk bonnet for Ma, too. I'll show them.

She laughed at herself then, at herself and at her brothers. What chance did any of them have of earning the reward? It was all big talk.

"Come on, you slowpokes," she said. "I'll race you to the raft."

"Pa's got company," said Luke as the others caught up with him.

A tall, broad-shouldered man stood on the bank, talking earnestly to Pa. He wore a slouch hat and he was clutching an old traveling bag.

When Pa called out to the family the visitor turned, and Serena saw that although he certainly was man-sized, he was still a boy, not much older than Luke.

"I'd surely be glad of a ride downriver, sir," he was saying.

Pa scratched his head. "I got no objection to accommodatin' you, young feller, but a boat-store is slow goin'. A steamboat'd be a lot quicker."

"Oh, time doesn't matter," the young man assured him. "And — and I can't spare the money for the boat fare. I'd be happy to work my way, work the sweep or help pole or whatever you need."

"Don't really even need help," said Pa. "Me'n the boys can handle it."

"Oh please, sir! I've got to get out of Brownsville right away. I've just *got* to!"

Pa chuckled. "You're in a hurry for a feller who says time doesn't matter. Oh, all right then. Come aboard. Lucinda, looks like we got us a passenger."

5

The Mysterious Passenger

THE STRANGER SCRAMBLED on and then gave his free hand to help Ma and Sweet Harmony. Serena had jumped aboard while they were talking, but Luke and Newtie stood there, looking at each other.

"Come on, boys, cast off! We can't wait here all day, you know. There's folks waitin' for us, and business to be done."

"Pa — " Newtie began, but Luke jabbed an elbow in his ribs.

"Cast off," said Luke. "We'll talk about it later."

Moments later they were in midstream, slipping past the busy town.

For a few minutes Pa and Ma were too busy to be sociable, Pa heaving on the sweep oar to steer away from

all the river traffic, Ma settling Sweet Harmony down
for her nap. Luke and Newtie's job was to coil the tie-
ropes neatly to be ready for the next landing. Nobody
had time to talk, but their visitor didn't seem to be much
of a talker. He was sort of shy, Serena thought. He
edged around to the far side of the shanty and stayed
there peering back at the town from around the corner
of the cow pen.

After a while he seemed to feel more at home, and by
the time Brownsville was out of sight behind them he
said to Pa, "If you want, I'll take the sweep, sir."

Luke said quickly, "Yes, Pa. Do you good to get a rest.
We could sit and . . . talk."

Pa laughed. "By ginger, I've done nothing but rest this
afternoon. Why don't you three boys catch us a mess of
fish for supper? Luke and Newtie, fix a line for — what
did you say your name was, son?"

"John. John Bun — Fenton."

Luke and Newtie gave each other one of those strange
looks. What were they up to? Then Luke said, "I'm Luke
Dowell, and this is Newtie. Here, give me your bag and
I'll stow it away. Then we can fish."

John Fenton hugged the bag closer to him. "N-no," he
said. "I like to keep it close. It's valuable. It's — it's all
I've got."

"Can't fish with your arms full, John," said Ma. "And
if we get caught in a steamboat wash it'll slip overboard.
Let me put it away in the shanty."

John handed over the bag after hesitating for a moment. Ma added with a laugh, "You don't need to be

fearful for it. None of us are planning to run away and disappear."

John flushed a deep brick red, but he said nothing.

Luke and Newtie looked at each other.

"Here," said Newtie quickly, "take Serena's pole. She can cut another at the next stop."

Ma saw Serena start to bristle and said gently, "He's our guest, Serena. We're supposed to make guests welcome."

Well, maybe, but why did it have to be her pole? Serena sat there all prickly with resentment as the three of them baited their hooks. With her worms, the worms she had dug that morning on the riverbank.

They didn't have much to say. They sat there watching for the sign of a nibble and never a word was said. Serena was determined not to be left out entirely, so she sat near, listening, but there wasn't anything to hear. Finally Luke said, "Where're you from, John? Where're you headed?"

There was a pause, and then John Fenton stammered, "A farm — back a ways, and I'm bound for downriver."

"Good thing," said Luke, "That's the only way this raft goes. You got work waiting for you?"

"N-no. I guess you'd say I got me a bad case of the yonders. I — I want to see some of the world."

They heard the blast of a boat horn then. Serena turned to see a flatboat with six oarsmen coming up rapidly behind them. The flatboat steered wide to go around the slower-moving raft. All the Dowells shouted and waved. It was still something of a novelty to meet another craft on what was turning out to be a busy river.

John Fenton didn't wave. He got up and hurried to the far side of the shanty, the shady side where Harmony was supposed to be napping.

"I thought I heard the little one cry," he said to Ma.

Ma laughed. "You mustn't fret yourself over Sweet Harmony. I can tell when she's yellin' for mad and when she's yellin' for pleasure. That was a pure pleasure yell. She liked seein' the boat go by, same as the rest of us."

Serena didn't think the new boy was so crazy to see the boat go by. He kept his head down and didn't even look up as the rivermen waved and called.

He was an odd one, she decided. But her two brothers weren't far behind him in odd behavior. They sat there nudging each other and whispering, too busy to notice that Newtie's line was bobbing. Serena reached over and grabbed the pole. Over Newtie's loud protest she landed a nice-sized catfish.

"One of us'll have fish for supper, anyway," she said. "I don't know about you two." She stamped off, leaving them suddenly very busy with their fishing.

Business was slow at the next stop. Perhaps it was too late in the afternoon, or perhaps the settlement was too near the shops of Brownsville. The folks gathered at the sound of the boat horn, all right, and they looked politely at the things Pa held up, but that was all. No one reached into a pocket to buy.

"A nice clock?" Pa suggested. "Real Bohea tea, a bargain! How about this fine iron kettle, now? I'm open to trade, friends. Have you extra butter, or wood ashes, or skins?"

"Who needs lamp oil?" Ma called out. No one did. Pa told a good story he had heard upriver, about a horse and an alligator. They all laughed heartily, and still no one bought.

"Dagnab it," Serena muttered to Newtie, "what are they waiting for?"

"Something for nothing. That's what they're waiting for, Tag-along."

"Don't call me Tag-along!" She kept her voice low, for Pa and Ma wouldn't stand for bickering in public.

Newtie was still smarting at the way she had hauled in his fish. "Maybe you could do a stunt to stir 'em up, like catching a whale. How about it, Tag? Show off a little."

"Oh!" She wanted to push him, and didn't dare. She wanted to show him. Something for nothing, he had said. Well, why not? She reached for the basket of buttons.

"Something for nothing!" she called. "One free button to each lady! Here's yours, Ma'am. Best pewter, newest design. Here you are, ma'am, brass, and it shines up like gold — "

"What good is only one button?" said a bearded man standing on the bank.

"Buy five more like it and you have a set," said Serena.

"Well!" said the surprised lady with the brass button.

"Well!" said Ma, just as surprised.

"Well! Well and good!" said Pa. "Spoken like a true storekeeper. See how nice your free button will look on this blue serge, ma'am. And five more to go with it? Yes indeed. Serena, help this customer find five more to match."

Before they were through they had sold the serge as well as the buttons. Pa got rid of two ready-made shirts that Ma had been sure he'd be stuck with — who in the world would *buy* a shirt? — and a handful of spoons and three porringers. The bearded man decided he was in the mood to barter, and Pa ended up with several more muskrat skins.

"That was a right smart idea, Serena," Pa said later as he counted the coins in the strongbox. "That was what I call real bamboozlement. Somethin' for nothin'. It sure turned things around, put folks in the mind of buying, didn't it? Next time we can't get things movin' we'll bamboozle the men with a cut of Pigtail tobaccy. Somethin' for nothin'!" He chuckled.

John Fenton had watched the storekeeping with interest, although he kept well out of the way.

"You do a good business, sir," he said to Pa. "I hope you hide your strongbox in a safe place. Not everyone on the river is honest. It'd be mighty tempting to some I've heard of."

Pa grinned. "I keep my gun handy," he said, and went on counting his muskrat skins.

Luke and Newtie looked at each other — a long, meaningful look. Now what were those two up to? Serena had a feeling it had something to do with John

Fenton, but she couldn't figure what. Oh well, she'd find out sooner or later.

The chore of winding the six wall clocks each night had fallen to Serena. Luke had said, "She'll forget. Better let me do it," but she had insisted. So far she hadn't skipped a single night, and she mentioned that every so often just so the boys would notice.

The clocks were friendly and noisy, click-clacking away, all telling a different time. She hoped they wouldn't sell them all. It would be nice to have one hanging on the wall of the farmhouse, when they found their farm and when they got the house built.

That night she forgot the clock winding for the first time. She was already in bed, stretched out on her hay-bag next to Sweet Harmony, when she remembered.

Drat! She'd have to creep out of bed in the dark and run the risk of waking Harmony. For a moment she considered going off to sleep and letting the clocks run down, but she decided against that. Luke and Newtie would jump at the chance to rub it in. Confuse and confound!

She groaned a little, threw back the blanket, and rolled silently out of bed. Sweet Harmony didn't stir. Thank goodness for that.

There was enough light in the sky to show her the shanty wall, and she groped along it for the door. It opened silently on its leather hinges and she went inside, feeling for the boxes and barrels stacked on the floor.

The clocks were still going, like sleepy crickets. It was

not hard to find the hook where the clock keys hung. As she reached out she heard voices, right through the chinks in the log shanty. Pa and Luke and Newtie must be leaning against it. They were keeping their voices quiet, but she was so close, only a log's width away, that she could hear every word.

"Don't you see, Pa," Luke was saying urgently, "there's something funny about his story."

"He never came from a farm," Newtie added. "He's pale as a fish belly, and his hands are soft."

"Now, now," Pa's deeper voice put in. "Don't get so excited, you two. Just because a feller doesn't come right out with his story doesn't mean he's a bank robber."

Bank robber? What were they talking about? Serena knew it wasn't good manners to listen to a private conversation. Ma had told her that more than once. But her natural curiosity got the best of her. Who was the bank robber?

"Put it all together, Pa. Why else would he hang onto that valise so tight? And why did he stammer and stutter when you asked his name? An honest man could speak out his name plain and clear, seems like."

"Quiet! He may not be asleep yet."

They were talking about John Fenton! Luke and Newtie thought he was one of the Brownsville robbers!

"You're makin' a mighty serious claim, boys, and all you've got is a few suspicions. I don't know as I like that. I'll agree to keep an eye on things, I'll go as far as that, but no further. Now get to sleep, both of you."

The voices faded away. When Serena was sure they

had all gone, she wound the clocks and crept back to her haybag.

This was certainly something to think about. And if Luke and Newtie had any fancy ideas about capturing a robber and claiming the reward, they'd better include her. For once she was not going to be left out.

6

The Ring-tailed Roarers

SUMMER WEATHER had begun with a rush even though it was only May. It felt like July, Ma said, and she did her best to make Serena and Sweet Harmony keep their sunbonnets on.

Pa lay on his haybag in the sun and played on his mouth organ between stops. Ma and Serena hummed along as they peeled the potatoes for dinner. After a while even John Fenton joined in. He may be a bank robber, thought Serena, but he's a likable one.

By now they were making as many as five or six stops a day.

"Some of these places aren't more'n a mile or two apart," Pa marveled. "The country's fillin' up. Folks're beginnin' to crowd up against each other somethin' dreadful. We did the right thing to move on, Lucinda. I'm sure of it."

"Well," Ma said. She didn't say it sharply, but it was plain she wasn't yet convinced. "I sort of like to see the houses close together, climbing up the hill from the river. Might be nice to look out and see the smoke of someone else's chimney, know there was a neighbor near."

"That's too close for comfort, to my way of thinkin'," said Pa. "I like a little elbow room."

At each stop Ma scouted the territory, scooping up a handful of dirt to see if it was rich enough, studying the lay of the land, looking for their new farm. She looked at the log houses and barns and questioned the settlers who came down to the riverbank to trade.

"Not yet," she always said. "Not yet, but soon."

Ma and Serena sloshed their clothes in the clear river water and hung them on the clothesline Luke rigged up on the roof. No hauling of buckets of water from the spring, no lugging baskets of wet wash to the clearing. Even Ma enjoyed the new kind of washday.

The banks of the river rose high and rocky on either side for miles, so when she spotted a place where there seemed to be a level meadow, Ma said, "Henry, can't we stop here? We should pasture Lilybelle for a while. The poor thing is perishin' for some fresh grass. We haven't seen a flat spot for a long time. Nothin' but hills and rocks, and no tellin' when we'll come to another."

"Not until we're clear out of the mountains, I reckon," agreed Pa. "From what Hawkins said, we've got a while before that. So heave ho, boys, we'll pull over and stop here."

Pa and John grabbed poles and Luke steered with the sweep oar, and in a short time they were tied up to a big water-willow.

"Don't let Lilybelle off her tether," Ma warned them. "She's a contrary thing, as contrary as Sweet Harmony. If once she got away we'd never get her back." Then she added, "And while you're pasturin' her, fetch a load of cook-wood, for we're gettin' low again."

Luke took Lilybelle's rope, Newtie picked up the ax, and they started up the bank. John hesitated. He looked as if he wanted to go along, but Luke and Newtie gave him no encouragement.

"Serena, you and John look for greens. Take Harmony, too, let her run a mite. The poke should be plentiful now. Pick it small and don't mislay my good knife."

Ma handed Serena a basket and a knife and they jumped ashore. It was a good day for hunting greens. It was a good day for anything, really. Maybe it was a good day for getting acquainted with their visitor.

Serena tried, but John was a hard one to get talking. "You miss farm life, John?"

"Farm life? Oh, farm life. No, I can't say that I do."

"Ma does," Serena confided. "She misses it every day. She's fretting now because it's time to plant and she has no garden to plant in."

John wasn't much of a talker, but he was a good listener. Before the basket was half full of poke he had heard the whole story of the traded farm and the Floating Emporium.

Drat! thought Serena. I got this all turned around. He's the one who knows all about us and I haven't found out a thing — except that he's got sharp eyes.

John had discovered a nest of young rabbits under a clump of blackberry brambles.

"Look at their ears," he said to Harmony. "Soft and fine as velvet." He put the brambles back carefully. "Their mother's nearby," he guessed, "probably shivering in her fur for fear we'll harm them."

He didn't sound much like a reckless bank robber to Serena. But that was probably what bank robbers were like. Tricky. Well, she could be tricky too, once she'd figured out how.

Ma came up the hill to meet them. She took Sweet Harmony's hand and said, "That's a fine mess of greens, thank you both. The boys've gone for one more load of kindlin', and then we'll be pullin' out."

"I'll help them carry the wood back," said John eagerly, and he loped off across the little field. An idea came to Serena then, an idea so underhand and tricky she was almost ashamed to think it.

"And I'll take the basket back, Ma," she offered. "You and Harmony can enjoy the dry land a mite longer."

She scrambled down the riverbank and jumped on the raft. Pa was whistling happily on the roof as he tossed fresh straw down into Lilybelle's stall. This was Serena's chance, before anyone came back.

She unfastened the shanty door and scooted inside, leaving it open to let in a little light. Now to find John's valise. If he was one of the Brownsville robbers, she'd soon know. The bag would be stuffed with money, surely. Where had Ma put it? She finally found it behind a molasses barrel. It was well wedged in but she managed to drag it out.

She was fumbling with the catch when the square of sunlight vanished. Someone had come in behind her.

"Serena!"

Pa's voice manged to be shocked and stern and angry all at the same time. "Serena Dowell! Were you plannin' to open that bag, that you know doesn't belong to you?"

"I — I — " she stammered.

"You've been bitten by the same suspicious bug as your brothers," Pa said sadly.

"If he is a bank robber, shouldn't we try to find out?"

"Not by pokin' and pryin' where we've got no right. I'd prefer to trust folks, Serena, not suspicion 'em without reason. Mistrust spoils things, child."

"But I want to *know*."

"Time has a way of workin' things out. Can't you try to be a little more like your name, Serena? Can't you go along quiet and easy and let things happen when they will?"

She thought that one over, and then said honestly, "I reckon you and Ma named me all wrong, Pa. I don't want to be serene all the time. I like a chance to stir things up and make 'em happen."

"All the same, it's a good name, and a good idea.

Gives you somethin' to aim for, don't you see? Try, anyway, Serena," he urged. "And about this bank robber thing, keep in mind that suspicion and mistrust sours things, casts a cloud — "

There was a shout and a scramble then. The rest were all coming back with Lilybelle.

"Quick!" said Pa. "Put John's bag back, and we'll say no more about it for now."

The day went along much as usual, but some of the sparkle had gone out of the sunshine. Serena went through her storekeeping chores without pleasure and was glad when the long day was almost over. Pa was right. Mistrust did spoil things.

There was more to see now that they were in deeper water. Flatboats were plentiful, three or four an hour. And they saw their first keelboat. It seemed to flash by the slow-moving raft, with twelve oarsmen hurrying it along.

"Sure makes good time, doesn't it?" asked Luke admiringly.

"Sure does. What makes it a keelboat, anyway?" asked Newtie.

Pa pushed back his hat and scratched his head. "Not bein' a riverman except by accident, I don't know all the names they give to boat parts. Now, a flatboat is no more'n a fancied-up raft. Rides on top of the water and carries its cargo all on top. But a keelboat, now, it has a section under the water, with cargo in it, grains or skins or suchlike. Judgin' from the ones I saw bein' built in Brownsville, I'd say the sides of a keelboat come to sort of a ridge at the bottom. Makes it ride the water easier, I reckon."

John nodded. "That's about it," he said. "That's the way a keelboat is built."

"From the whiff I got of that one, I'd say skins was what they were carrying down below."

Newtie sniffed. "I'd rather carry the skins out in the air until they're cured," he said, looking over his shoulder at the muskrat skins nailed to the side of the shanty. "A raft suits me fine."

"Suits me too," said Pa. "I got no need for racin'. I'm content just to drift along and enjoy it. Until we find our farm, of course."

They were tied up for supper when a splashing and shouting on the river startled them all.

"Hoo-ee! Heave 'er over! Lean on 'er! Pull, pull, you lazy devil, pull!"

A flatboat swung around and scraped alongside the Floating Emporium. The man who was giving the orders bellowed, "Break out your rum and tobaccy, for we've run plumb outta both and we're mean as red-hot snappin' turtles!"

Pa stood up with his soup bowl in his hand. "We're havin' us a bite of supper, gentlemen, but we'll open up for business as soon as we're done here."

The other man laid the sweep oar aside and stepped over onto the raft. "Reckon you don't understand, storekeeper. We're ring-tailed roarers! We ain't called Roarin' Ralph and Beefy Bullnose for nothin'. We're regular screamers! We can outshoot, outbrag, outdrink

and outfight any man on both sides of the river, and rarin' to do it! Now bring out the rum and 'baccy, like Beefy said. Don't keep us waitin' or we'll tear your raft to kindling and feed you to the fishes!"

Ma gasped and pulled Sweet Harmony and Serena close to her.

"Now, now," said Pa soothingly. "What's a matter of a few minutes between friends? Like I said, we'll be through here in due time. Set yourselves down and cool off your tongues, for I don't appreciate rough talk in front of my wife and young 'uns."

Serena felt sick to her stomach. These were the kind of rivermen Mr. Hawkins had warned them about. "Don't rile up a ring-tailed roarer," he had said. "They're poison."

Beefy Bullnose shouted, "Why, you scrawny little pie-face! I've got me a barbed-wire tail, and I don't give a dang where I drag it! We'll help ourselves!"

They started for the shanty. Luke got to his feet. His voice was shaky, for one of the big men would make three of him, but he said, "Stop right there, stranger. We'll open up the store when we're ready, like my Pa said." Newtie was standing too, right by Luke's side.

Beefy looked at the two kids standing there by Pa and grinned. "Well, looka here, Ralph. The young 'uns have got no more manners than the old man."

He took a step toward them. It seemed to Serena as if time were standing still. Any instant now the men would knock Pa and the boys down. Then she heard

John's voice from around the corner of the shanty. He had Pa's gun pointed at Beefy.

"Don't make a move," he said.

"Why you yearling catamount! I'll bend that firin' piece over your head and make it ring like a bell!"

"Bell?" sang out Sweet Harmony. "Bell!"

She had been listening to all that had gone on and this was the only word she understood. In a flash she broke away from Ma's grasp. Serena and Ma grabbed for her but Harmony was already out of their reach. Moving fast, she zipped between John and Beefy, asking happily, "Where my bell?"

She scuttled along, going like a streak. Her tether caught around Beefy's leg as she doubled back behind Ralph. Both looked down, startled. That moment of hesitation was enough.

Serena plunged forward and grabbed Beefy around the knees. Beefy was spun off balance, and Newtie gave him the extra push that shoved him to the deck. Pa and Luke swarmed all over Ralph and half-pushed, half-wrestled him down. Ma trampled over all of them in her hurry to reach Harmony. John stood over the two surprised rivermen shouting. "Don't make a move or I'll blow you to kingdom come!"

The confusion was terrible. Sweet Harmony was screaming her loudest in the tangled center of things, and Ma was screeching, "Let her loose! Let our sweet baby loose!"

The two big rivermen had had enough.

"Shove off, Ralph," shouted Beefy. "Let's get out of here!"

But Serena was still hanging on to his knees, and he couldn't get to his feet.

"Shove 'em off, Newtie," John yelled. "Give their boat a push!"

Newtie shoved at the bobbing flatboat, and as the ring-tailed roarers struggled to get to their feet Pa and Luke rolled them over and over right to the edge of the raft. They went off into the water with a mighty splash. Clawing and sputtering, they began to swim after the flatboat that was already moving briskly down the river.

The Dowells and John Fenton laughed and laughed. They whooped, they gasped. Just when they thought they were all laughed out, someone would say, "Where my bell?" and they'd start up again.

"By ginger!" said Pa weakly, wiping his eyes on his shirttail. "By ginger and jiminy! I'd have liked to be standin' by, watchin' that fight. Didn't go according to any of the rules, but we won, anyway, even if we did do ourselves out of a sale."

"That was right quick-witted of you to grab the gun, John," Ma said.

"I don't know if I could have shot them, Mrs. Dowell. I don't know if I could have pulled the trigger."

Pa grinned at him. "Don't really make any difference," he said. "You had the right spirit, boy, but the gun wasn't loaded. We just bamboozled them. Bamboozlement is better'n shootin' any day."

7

The Rescue

T WAS PEACEFUL on the river. They drifted along, making a stop at each little group of houses, then drifting some more. They saw an ark, a big clumsy square house taking up the whole raft, large enough for real living space for a whole family of settlers, even indoor stabling for the animals.

"Nice and cozy if it rains," Ma approved.

"Mighty hard to steer, I reckon," said Pa. "Look how the tail end swings when the current grabs it. Takes a lot of steering to keep it on course. As for the rain, we're neither sugar nor salt, rain won't spoil us. The few little showers we've had haven't hardly wet us through."

"That won't last forever," predicted Ma. "If it does, the crops're in trouble. I never in my life saw such a dry springtime. Oh, look there!"

The folks on the ark had run aground on a shoal.

"Need any help?" Pa shouted.

The man on the ark said it happened to them every mile or so, and they'd be able to pole off, thank you. Sure enough, before the Floating Emporium rounded the next bend they had shoved the ark into deeper water.

After that there seemed to be nothing happening at all. Birds chirped in the trees. Pa was almost dozing at the sweep. Luke and Newtie and John and Serena fished, but without too much interest.

After a while Serena laid her pole aside and went to help Ma hem the ruffle on her new dress. Sweet Harmony played close by. She had wrapped her doll in the scraps of pink and was talking happily to herself.

Ma yawned. "I guess we all needed a mite of quiet after all the excitement we had yesterday."

John had grown tired of fishing too and wandered restlessly around the raft. Finally he said to Ma, "I'd like to get something from my bag, ma'am."

"I put it in the shanty," she said, "jammed behind the molasses barrel."

He went into the shanty and came out with a bound ledger book, a quill pen, and an ink pot. He settled down not far from Ma with his back braced against the wall.

Dip, scratch, dip, scratch, dip, scratch.

"What's he up to?" Serena whispered.

Ma said, "He's writing a letter, most like. He'll tell us if he wants us to know."

Serena got up several times and sauntered past as if to check on her untended fishing line, but she couldn't tell what the tall boy was doing. Newtie had said he was pale as a fish belly, but that was no longer true. Several days of river sun had burned his face and arms to a bright pink. His hands had blistered from chopping wood. Soon he'd be so brown and toughened you'd hardly know he was the same person.

Maybe that's what he had in mind, thought Serena. Maybe the boys are right, and he's got a good reason for wanting to look like a different person.

Well, whatever he was doing, he liked it. He grunted and held out the page, looking at it intently with a smile on his face.

"I've caught it. Looks to me like I've caught it," he murmured to himself.

"You've caught what?" Serena wanted to know. He fanned the ink dry and snapped the ledger book closed, but not before Serena had gotten a quick peek at the pages.

"It's Ma! It's Ma and Sweet Harmony and me! Oh, let me see, let me see! Ma, look here!"

"By dabs! That's me, right down to the last hair. And there's Serena, and the baby! John, you did this with your own hand?"

He nodded, both bashful and proud.

Serena looked down at the drawing. There was Ma, settled down on her haybag with the folds of calico spread on her lap. Serena was basting away on the long ruffle, her eyes intent on the stitching. Harmony's tum-

bled curls were as real as real. Even the battered old cornhusk doll seemed real.

"I can't believe it," marveled Ma. "I've heard about things like this, but I never thought to see it. Henry" — she raised her voice — "come here. John's done something here that you should see."

Pa and the boys inspected the drawing in open-mouthed wonder.

"Son, that's a pure prettiment. You've got a natural bent for it. I hear there are fellers who do this for a livin', takin' off folks' likenesses. You ever think about that?"

"It's all I do think of, day and night. And I've figured out a way I can learn, but it takes money."

"I can see where it might," said Pa.

"I aim to get the money. I don't care how," said John fiercely.

"Well, now," said Pa. "You shouldn't go so far as to say that — "

"I don't care *how*," John repeated. "I don't care what it takes. I don't aim to let *anything* stand in my way now. I've taken the first big step, and I'll do whatever else I have to do."

Pa looked at him uneasily, with a worried frown, but he didn't press John for anything more.

After that John drew all day long, whenever he wasn't helping with the chores. Each one of the Dowells sat for a likeness, and he drew Lilybelle and the pigs too, and the hens scratching around on the roof.

He was always pleased when they praised his work, when they let him know they thought it was quite a wonderful thing to be doing. But when Ma asked where he had learned and Pa wanted to know his plans for the future, he had nothing to say.

"He's an odd one," said Luke. "I can't figure him out. I never thought you could be a robber and an artist too."

Newtie shrugged. "You heard him say he'd do *anything* to get the money he needs. Maybe some people can be two things at one time, good and bad. I'm still keeping an eye on him."

As they drew nearer to Pittsburgh the traffic on the river got heavier.

"Those dagnabbed steamboats'll run us down," Pa complained. "It isn't natural for folks to have to go so fast. We'd better stay close to shore. Keep a sharp eye out for trees and rocks, boys, and shout me a warning if you see anything."

They heard the steamboat whistle in the distance. Pa steered over to give her plenty of room to pass. None of them were prepared for what happened next.

The boat came charging from behind a little island and cut across suddenly quite close to the bank, probably to avoid a snaggle of fallen trees.

It roared past them only a few feet away. The captain saw the raft almost too late. The bell clanged wildly, the whistle screamed again, the spray from the paddle wheel drenched them. The steamboat passed so close Serena could look right up into the startled faces of the passengers at the rail.

Pa sprang for the sweep oar, Luke and Newtie shouted and shook their fists at the steamboat, and

John — John gasped, "Uncle Matthew! He's found me out! He saw me!"

A man at the rail stared, pointed, opened his mouth, but his shout was drowned in the noise of the whistle.

A second later they were caught in the churning wash. The raft shivered and dipped crazily. Pa clung to the sweep while Luke staggered across the deck to help him. Everything in the shanty fell with a crash. Ma had risen to her knees as the whistle startled her, and she tumbled over with her sewing basket spilled around her. Serena clung to Ma.

There was so much clatter and confusion that no one thought about Sweet Harmony. One minute she was playing happily at the end of her rope, and in the next instant they saw that the rope had come loose. With a shriek Ma grabbed for her and missed. The raft tipped again. Sweet Harmony was tossed into the water and disappeared into the churning foam of the steamboat's wake.

For one terrible instant everything stayed the same. The animals went on protesting, Pa and the boys struggled with the sweep, Ma fought to get her balance, and Serena clung there, frozen.

Then John let out a whoop. He hit the water just as Harmony's head bobbed out of the foam. In a second he reached her, but a rolling wave washed her out of his reach. Pa and Luke wrenched the long sweep oar out of the oarlock and ran with it. They stretched it out just as John grabbed again for the little girl. This time he got a grip on her dress and a grip on the oar and held fast. Ma and Serena and Newtie flung themselves on the oar to hold it steady, and Pa jumped in.

It seemed like ages, but it was all over in a flash. Pa handed Harmony up to Ma's outstretched arms. Luke and Newtie hauled Pa and John aboard the raft.

Afterwards, Ma and Serena and Newtie bawled like babies, they were so relieved. Poor frightened Lilybelle mooed, the pigs grunted and squealed, the hens squawked, and what did Sweet Harmony do? She choked and sputtered, and then she laughed.

Pa looked at her and shook his head. "Well, I'll be ramsquaddled. We always said she was so contrary if she fell in the river she'd float upstream, and danged if she didn't try it!"

Ma stopped crying and blew her nose. "This child doesn't take kindly to peace and quiet. Never has, never will. Come on, all of you, into dry clothes, and then I'll fix us up a treat to celebrate."

*

"Excitement does give me an appetite," said Pa as he put honey on one more of Ma's cornmeal biscuits. "I got me a bottomless pit and I can't seem to fill it up. Here, John, have another."

John shook his head. He had hardly touched his supper.

Ma said gently, "You did a brave deed today, John. Don't think because we're all laughin' and crackin' jokes we don't thank you for what you did. We'll never forget that, not one of us, and we'll tell the story to Harmony soon as she's old enough to take it in. It was a good day for all of us when you came aboard at Brownsville."

John said sadly, "You don't know what I've done. If you knew you wouldn't say that."

Serena burst out, "John Fenton, I don't care what you've done! I'll always be glad we met you, even if you are a bank robber!"

There. She had said right out what some of the others were thinking.

"Serena!" said Pa sternly. "Serena, hold your tongue!"

John turned to look at her.

"Bank robber? What — why? Serena, what makes you think I'm a bank robber?"

"I just don't care! You rescued Harmony, that's enough for me. I won't turn you in to the law, and I won't touch one penny of the reward money, so there!"

No one said anything. John seemed to be too surprised to speak. Finally Pa said, "Appears like it is time for some explanations. By ginger, it's high time we got things cleared up. John, you begin. Who are you? Where do you come from? Why did you have to leave Brownsville in such a hurry? And who was the man on the steamboat — you called him Uncle Matthew, I recall. What *has* your Uncle Matthew found out?"

8

The Gentlemen Travelers

'M PLANNING to leave at the next stop, sir. It's better if I go on to Pittsburgh on foot."

"John, we're set up to be your friends, but we've got to know the truth. Who was the fellow on the steamboat? Is he someone you've wronged?"

"I might as well tell it, I guess, though you won't think well of me for it. I reckon I've wronged my uncle by running away like this, but he's wronged me wicked, and I'll never go back to him, never! Not even if he gets the law on me. I won't go back!"

"Sounds to me like you'd better start at the beginnin'. He's got some claim on you, this uncle of yours?"

"He's my legal guardian, no blood relation. He's my mother's sister's husband. When my ma and pa died three years ago, Uncle Matthew and Aunt Julia took me in. He made himself my guardian, all signed and sealed.

He signed and sealed me to be an apprentice, too, a clerk in his bank. He said if I do well, when I serve out my years I'm to go in with him in the Bunby businesses."

"Doesn't sound so wicked yet."

"He's a hard, sour man, my uncle. He changed my name from Fenton to Bunby, and he swore he'd wipe every trace of my father's shiftless ways out of me. Pa wasn't shiftless. He was a traveling painter, and a good one. We didn't have a regular home, but we were a family, my mother and father and I. Just like you Dowells are, a traveling family. We didn't have a settled house either, but we were doing fine and aiming for better things. Then my folks took the fever, and after that I had to go and live with the Bunbys. I haven't had a family since."

Ma said, "Ah," and John rushed on.

"Oh, they didn't beat me or anything like that. Everything was all proper that way. But there's no bend in either of them. They just don't understand. Uncle Matthew said I had to forget my old ways, I had to change. He said he'd never stand for another artist in the family, and he burned all my father's canvases and paints."

John had a kind of sob in his voice and he had to clear his throat before he went on.

"I draw all the time anyway — I can't help myself — but I have to sneak it. I don't want to clerk in an office, not even if I'm a rich clerk someday. Never to use a pen for anything but adding up figures. Never even get out-

[77]

side except when I'm taking the payroll down to the boat shop or the sawmill. Uncle Matthew owns half of Brownsville now, and he aims to own the other half and own me too. Well, not if I can help it. Mr. Dowell, if I can't be an artist like my father, I'll do something desperate, I tell you."

"When you're of age you'll own your own time. As soon as you turn twenty-one you can do what you please," said Pa thoughtfully.

"But that's seven years off, and every year of learning counts."

"Well, boy, I can't rightly advise you to keep on runnin'. Wouldn't be right, the law is the law. But I can't rightly advise you to put away your dream, neither. I tell you, when a fellow finds out what he is meant for, what he does best, he'd oughta stick to it no matter what. Sometimes the chance doesn't come around twice."

They had all been so engrossed in John's story that they weren't watching the riverbank. Newtie looked up suddenly and said, "Pa, we're coming to a good-sized settlement. Do we pull over for a landing?"

"Dagnab it!" exclaimed Pa. "Just when we were gettin' down to cases. John, promise me you won't go ashore yet. Not until we've had a chance to talk some more. Maybe there's a way we can bamboozle your Uncle Matthew. I'm a great believer in bamboozlement."

"Pull in, Pa. Blow the horn, Serena."

Confuse and confound! Serena said to herself. Just when we were getting to the good part.

"I'll get out the seeds," Ma said. "Time for folks to be puttin' in their garden patches. I know I would, were we settled on dry land right now."

Ma was right. Folks were ready for seeds, but then they were ready for almost anything. Whetstones, grindstones, buttons, needles, pins, hand mirrors, clocks. Pa and Ma measured off dress goods and weighed out spices and tea and tobacco.

A man with three coonskins had his heart set on a copper teakettle, but Pa stuck and hung until the man made it four skins and a bag of wool.

"Your pa's the best bargainer ever lived," whispered Ma proudly to Serena. "It certainly pleasures him to trade."

All the time Pa was laughing and joshing with the customers, they were joshing back and buying almost anything he held up. Nobody wanted to leave.

Finally only two customers were left. They both wore what had once been fancy clothes, but they looked pretty much the worse for wear, rumpled and not too clean. One of them, the one with the red flowered waistcoat and the scar on his face, said, "You got anything for blistered feet, mister? My friend here could use some."

"I got the best little remedy in the world. Good for blisters and corns and sore feet generally. Also for aches and fevers, worn-out blood, weak limbs, and bilious shakes."

"Lorenzo's got all that, and then some."

"Then a tin of this Indian Panacea Salve will make a

new man of him, and of your mule too, if you've got a mule. Works just as well on beasts as on humans, they say. But I don't guess you've been doin' much mule ridin'. Looks like you and your friend have walked a mighty far piece in them fancy boots."

"Never mind how far we've walked," snarled Lorenzo.

"Easy, Lorenzo," said the first man. "This boat-store might turn out to be a blessing in disguise. You do a right smart trade, I perceive?" he said to Pa.

"Hard to do better," said Pa. "It's a good business if you've got the knack for it."

John tugged at Pa's sleeve, but Pa had started on one of his favorite funny stories, about a settler and a Yankee peddler who had the knack. John turned to Ma, but she was busy folding up the yards of calico.

"Luke," he said urgently, "I've got to tell you something."

"Sure," said Luke, "soon as I straighten up these spices. When business is good it sure makes a mess of the shelves."

"I'll listen," said Serena. "Tell me."

Desperately, John whispered. "Get word to your pa somehow! Tell him to watch out. Those men are the Brownsville robbers!"

Her mouth fell open. "How do you know?"

"Because I saw them, Serena. I was right there. I was part of the robbery!"

Pa was still talking to the last two customers.

"Yessir," the tall man was saying. "I can see you're a skilled trader. I can tell by the brisk business you're doing."

"Well," said Pa modestly. "I don't know as I'm so tarnation skilled, but I'll have to admit business is good, perishin' good."

"My friend and I are going into the boat-store business ourselves. Down on the Mississippi — we wouldn't interfere with your trade hereabouts, sir. But we lack experience in the storekeeping line."

His friend had take off his worn boots and was applying Indian Panacea to his blistered heels. He looked up, startled, and the other fellow gave him a sharp nudge with his boot.

"Isn't that right, Lorenzo? We're planning to have a boat-store?" He went on, "We'd surely take it kindly if you'd allow us to ride along with you and observe your persuasive method of dealing with the public."

Pa looked pleased. "That's mighty flatterin', gents. I reckon I could teach you a few tricks, come to think of it. We'd be pleased to have your company."

Serena tugged at his sleeve. "Pa, Pa!" Her whisper was urgent. "Pa!"

She had to think of an excuse for interrupting him. "John's took bad with something. He's got to talk with you."

She pulled at his coat, and as she led him away he called back, "Make yourselves comfortable, gentlemen."

[81]

As soon as they were on the other side of the shanty she said, "They aren't gentlemen, Pa. They're the Brownsville robbers."

"By ginger! Who says so?"

"I do," said John, keeping his voice very low. What he said in Pa's ear made Pa's eyes bug open.

"You're sure?"

"Dead sure," said John, "and I've got proof. Serena, see if you can get my bag out of the shanty. Don't let them notice."

In a moment she scooted back, her heart pounding. "They weren't paying me any mind. What's in it, John?"

"All I've got in the world." He sorted around among brushes and pencils, a couple of shirts, an extra pair of shoes, and found what he was looking for.

"Here," he said. "Right here."

It was a leather-bound ledger, every page filled with drawings instead of numbers and accounts. Drawings of people sitting and standing, walking, sawing, hammering, writing. Dogs, cats, ink pots, cooking kettles, and there, plain as day, Pa's "gentlemen." There was the thin dandified one with the scar down the side of his face, and the other one whose feet were sore.

Pa stared, and John explained. "I was at my desk in the bank — I told you I was my uncle's clerk — and three men came in with guns. They tied us up and cleaned us out, every penny, and packed the money in a valise. Then they hightailed it down toward the river. As soon as they left I started working on the knots until I got loose. Then I drew their pictures as clear as I could recall."

"By dabs! I've been bamboozled for fair! I've already invited the scoundrels to ride with us. If I try to turn them away now, it'll look suspicious."

John agreed. "If we go along with them and don't let on, we can wait for a chance to grab them. But watch out, they're bad ones through and through."

"They aren't carrying any valise — "

"I figure that's where the third one came in. He must have gone a different way, by boat maybe. There was a steamboat about ready to pull out. I remember hearing the warning whistle while I was getting untied. They might be planning to meet somewhere. Something was said, real quick, and I can't for the life of me remember what it was — "

"Do you think they'd recognize you?"

"They got a good look at me in the bank. I'll keep out of their way and not risk it."

"I'll give out that you're shy of strangers. You know, foolin' those vipers is goin' to be pure pleasurement. We'll hornswoggle them inside out." Pa thought for a moment. "Serena, you'll have to do a little play-actin'. Stick to them like mustard plaster and keep 'em talkin' while we explain things to Ma and the boys."

"But what'll I say?"

"Anything. Ask them questions about the Mississippi, anything you can think of. You got to do it, Serena. It mustn't look as if we suspected a thing. Act natural, as if nothin' was out of order."

Then Pa shouted, "Cast off! We're ready to go!"

Luke and Newtie untied the ropes and pushed the raft out where the current could catch it. A few moments later Pa called, "Give me a hand, boys. The sweep is snagged."

Serena knew it was time to do her part. She had to give Pa and John a chance to tell the boys. The lump in her throat felt as big as a bullfrog, but she walked right up to the strangers.

"M-my name is S-Serena," she stammered. "I — I wish you'd tell me about the M-Mississippi — " She sat down beside them and hid her trembling hands in her skirt. "I'd surely like to know all about the M-Mississippi — "

Once she got them going it wasn't too hard. The shorter one, Lorenzo, wasn't much for conversation, but the other one was a talker. With only a question now and then to prime the pump, he went on and on.

When Ma was finished in the shanty, Pa made an excuse to call her over. When she came back to start supper, she was walking stiff as a board and her eyes looked scared. But she said bravely, "Our supper won't be anything fancy, gentlemen, but I hope you'll share it with us."

Serena knew Ma knew, but the robbers never guessed. With a big sigh of relief, Serena got up to help her mother. Her part of the plan was over, at least for a time.

9

Gustus and Lorenzo Bamboozled

THEY USUALLY tied up for the night and then ate, but this time was going to be different. Pa said, "We'll eat on the run. We want to make as much time as we can before dark, so's we can reach Pittsburgh tomorrow."

Serena understood. John was at the sweep, and he'd have his supper there. By the time they tied up it would be too dark to see what he looked like.

All that afternoon and evening they held quick whispered conferences. First Ma and Newtie sat with the strangers, then Pa and Luke. They didn't leave them alone for a minute, didn't give them the chance to cook up any plans. Sweet Harmony stayed with them all the time. She rang her bell and staggered back and forth, trailing her tether. At last Lorenzo said, "Get outta here,

kid! Don't step on my feet one more time or I'll — "

His friend said quickly, "He's only joking, ma'am. She's a charming child. We're both of us lovers of children."

"I can see that." Ma smiled as if she meant it. "I can see that plain as day." She made no move to have Sweet Harmony play somewhere else.

Pa made quite a show of loading his gun. "One thing you must learn when you have your own boat-store, gentlemen. Not everybody on the river is to be trusted. I always sleep with my gun to hand, in case trouble starts."

Scarface, who had introduced himself as Gustus P. Wheeler, said, "A very sensible precaution. I hope you also keep your money box well hidden."

"No thieves'd ever find it. I keep it out of sight behind the spices."

Now why did Pa say that? Didn't he see that the robbers were trying to find out where he kept the money? He went right on visiting and joking just as if he hadn't let the cat out of the bag.

Serena thought she'd never be able to get to sleep. There was so much to think about, and all of it scary. She did, somehow, and the next thing she knew it was daylight.

"We won't stop to trade, will we?" she asked Luke first chance she got.

"We have to. We're a boat-store. It'd look funny if we went right past a settlement. We have to pretend that nothing is going on."

They tried to be bold about it, but it wasn't easy. Pa played his mouth organ as usual, and nodded to the others to sing. The tunes came out squawky. It was hard to keep up the play-acting. And when the customers came running down to the landing, it was harder than ever. Serena kept a bright smile plastered on her face. She smiled until her skin felt stretched.

Gustus P. Wheeler and Lorenzo smiled too. Every time Pa made another sale they looked at one another and grinned.

She could tell Pa was glad when it was over. He slid his heavy cash box carelessly behind the box of nutmegs and said, "You saw how we did it, gents. You'll find most of it is practice. Now let's sit here and visit. I believe we're less than ten miles out of Pittsburgh, and it appears to me we can make it easy today if we don't make too many stops. I want time to stock up on some new goods there, and I've a bit of business to do."

Serena drifted over to talk to John. Ma was already there with her mending. They talked very quietly.

"I figure the third one'll be waiting for them in town. The one who has the valise full of money."

Ma had John's sketchbook open at the drawings he had made after the robbery.

"He cuts a fine figure, I must say. A dandy. Almost too handsome. Almost — pretty, don't you think?"

John stared at the picture. "He had an odd walk. I noticed it especially. Like — like — " His voice trailed off as he thought. "Mrs. Dowell, what if the third one wasn't a man?"

"You mean a boy?"

"I mean a woman! What if the third robber got on the noon steamboat as a man, changed out of her men's clothes in a stateroom, and got off as a woman? Not a soul would suspect, not even if the law was searching every boat."

"Confuse and confound!" said Ma. "Did you hear her voice?"

"No, that one never spoke, just nodded. Even at the last . . . Now I recall, the tall one said something like, 'We'll meet you in paradise,' and even then he — or she — just nodded. Paradise. Isn't that odd?"

"That was a peculiar thing to say. What else?"

John shook his head. "I can't remember a thing. You see, I'd already made up my mind the night before that I was going to leave that day, and I had my bag packed. When there was all that commotion it seemed like a good time for me to light out. I was thinking mostly about that."

Ma stared at him. "It occurs to me that your Uncle Matthew might think you were in cahoots with the thieves, you leavin' at the same time and all."

"All I could think of was writing him a note and getting away. There's a stagecoach out of Pittsburgh for Philadelphia. I'm bound and determined to be on it."

"Philadelphia's a far piece."

"I'd go to the ends of the earth to get to where there are artists. I can find a painter who'll take me on as a helper, I know I can. I've got to. Someone who needs a strong fellow to sweep up his studio and build the fire and grind colors for paint. Someone who'll teach me things on the side. I'll do a good job for him. I'll work day and night."

"I wish you good fortune, John. But what about your uncle? Runnin' away from your legal guardian is a serious business, you know. He owns your time until you're twenty-one. He'll be waitin' in Pittsburgh to take you back."

John looked unhappy. "I reckon I'll have to figure that one out when the time comes."

There'll be a lot of things to figure out when the time comes, thought Serena. I only hope we can figure them all.

The day was endless. Dinner was over, the food put away, the dishes rinsed off in the river. There was nothing to do but wait. Ma kept climbing the ladder to fuss with the chickens. Luke and Newtie and Serena strung out their fishing lines and then wandered restlessly around the raft. John stayed busy at the sweep oar. Pa lounged in the sunshine and played his mouth organ. Slowly, steadily, the raft drifted downstream to Pittsburgh.

Serena whispered to Ma. "I've got the all-over fidgets. What's going to happen?"

Ma tried to smile. She had washed Sweet Harmony's grubby face and hands and put a clean smock on the little girl. Then she combed Serena's long brown hair.

"Don't you worry," she said, sounding worried herself. "Your pa is a pure wonderment at comin' up with ideas. He'll work it out, you'll see. Now sit still while I fix your braids."

Serena sat still but she didn't stop worrying.

Gustus P. Wheeler and Lorenzo were leaning against the wall of the shanty where Pa had piled a couple of haybags, saying, "Make yourself comfortable, gents. Sit upwind of the pigpen. You'll find the air sweeter."

Serena didn't see why he bothered about the comfort of those two men. She didn't care if they were miserable.

"Your pa knows what he's doin'," whispered Ma. "He's got them sittin' right where he can keep an eye on them. They can't make a move without his seein' it."

Ma took her mending and sat down beside Gustus and Lorenzo and motioned for Serena to follow. Luke and Newtie came over too.

They could hear Pa banging around in the shanty. He said he was putting away his gun. "No need for this now," he said in a loud voice. "We're comin' to the big city. I always make sure it's unloaded so's the little one won't get aholt of it. Can't be too careful with the dear little one."

Gustus looked around and smiled. The idea of an unloaded gun seemed to please him. Lorenzo made a sour face at the dear little one. Sweet Harmony had taken a real fancy to him. She sat close by him, singing and clanging her bell and banging on an iron skillet. Lorenzo scowled and pulled his hat over his ears.

There was a lot more traffic on the river than there had been before. Houses and barns were clustered much closer together on either side.

Suddenly Luke shouted, "Look, we're here! That must be Pittsburgh!"

There it was. Beyond the hills on either side, past the high riverbanks and the trees, the city stretched out in front of them.

"By dabs!" said Ma. "I never saw anything so crowded in all my days."

Horses and wagons clattered on the long wharves. Men shouted as they wrestled with barrels and bales. All kinds of boats, keelboats and flatboats and steamboats and rowboats, jostled their way to the landings. There were more people than the Dowells had ever seen before, and all crowded together, shoulder to shoulder. There was row after row of buildings.

"Pittsburgh," said Gustus. He rose and stretched and smoothed his flowered waistcoat. "Get ready, Lorenzo. It's almost time."

Lorenzo pulled on his boots. He winced as he stood up. "Ouch," he complained. "My feet are killing me. I don't see how I can walk."

"Shut up!" Suddenly Gustus wasn't smiley and polite anymore. "Keep 'em covered while I get the money from the shanty."

Both men had pulled out guns, and Lorenzo was pointing his right at them, right at Ma and her children.

"My gracious — " Ma began.

Lorenzo said to her, "You heard him. Shut up, and you too, you noisy little brat. No more of that racket!"

Harmony looked up and smiled at him. She gave her bell another clang. He snarled and snatched it out of her hand. It clanged and splashed and vanished in the river.

That was too much for Serena. She had never liked Lorenzo, and now she was so angry she didn't think. She grabbed Harmony's iron skillet and *thwack!* she slammed it down on Lorenzo's foot.

He let out a yell. In just the second that his gun wobbled, Luke and Newtie jumped him. He fell to the deck with a thump.

At the same time there was a shot, a crash, and a howl in the shanty. Ma said, "Never mind that, Pa's got him. Sit on Lorenzo's head, Serena." She reached in her mending basket and from under the stockings she pulled out a length of rope.

"There," she said, when they had Lorenzo tied securely. "I was ready for him. He's trussed as neat as a roasting fowl. He can't do any harm now. You sit on him, Newtie, while we go help Pa and John."

Lorenzo started to squawk. Ma jammed a stocking into his open mouth.

"No more of that racket. If he fusses, Newtie, give his feet another rap with the skillet."

Ma and Luke and Serena ran around to the back of the shanty. They found Pa holding his gun in Gustus P. Wheeler's ribs while John tied him up. The money box had been dumped on the floor and coins were scattered all over.

"Afraid there'll be some straightenin' to do in there, Lucinda. He dropped the strongbox when he went down."

"You shot him, Pa?"

"No, fired into the air and the noise surprised the wits out of him. Brought him to his knees as neat as if I'd hit him. He never figured on the gun's bein' loaded. That did it, that and the trip wire I fixed up. I figured one of them'd go inside for the money box just about as we landed."

Ma said to Serena, "You see? Your pa isn't big, but he's mighty. He fooled them about the gun, too. You saw how they grinned when they thought he had unloaded it. I guess they found out!"

Pa said, "By ginger, we bamboozled 'em. We outskunked the skunks! We ramsquaddled the robbers! All of us together. Now all we have to do is turn these varmints over to the law."

10

Mr. Matthew Bunby

A THOUGHT for a moment. "It'd be a sight easier if the law'd come to take the varmints off our hands here. One of us'll have to find where the constable's office is. Not you, John, I don't want your uncle to run into you afore we've got a plan worked out. Luke, I may need your help here. Newtie, you're the one. Ask around. Find the constable and hustle him back here as fast as you can."

"Pa — " Serena pleaded.

"All right, you too, Serena. With two of you, you won't get lost in the town. Hurry!"

"Come on, Tag-along," said Newtie importantly. "Step lively now. I don't intend to be held back by a girl dawdling along."

Serena didn't waste a moment in arguing. She scrambled up the steep ladder to the pier ahead of Newtie and raced across the rough planked wharf. Newtie pounded along a step or two behind her. As they passed a dock worker pushing a load of kegs, she said, "Please, sir, which way is the constable's office?" and Newtie panted, "Which way?"

The man shrugged and went trundling on about his work. A second worker had no better response, but the third man they questioned paused and wiped his brow.

"Up that street there." He pointed. "You can't miss it. Only three squares and turn to the — " His instructions were drowned out by the shouts of a dray driver. They jumped out of the way, and by the time the heavy wagon had rumbled past the man had picked up his load and started on.

"We can ask someone else," said Serena. "Come on!"

The confusion would have been frightening if they had had time to think about it. They were in such a hurry that they just ducked in and out of the traffic. They shoved past slow-moving men pushing barrows. They flattened themselves against a wall when a wagon clattered by and started off again as soon as it was past.

"Three squares," said Newtie. "We turn right at this corner."

"Left," said Serena. "He told us left. I heard him."

"I heard him too," argued Newtie. "I'm the oldest and I say turn right."

"Left. No time to fool around. I'll go this way and you try that."

"You'll get lost," he warned, but Serena had already

turned to the left and was darting up a narrow lane. She passed a cobbler's shop and a hatter. They were easy to spot. But what kind of a sign would a constable have?

"Look out, girl!" shouted a stout man as she barreled along. "Watch where you're going, shoving folks!"

She remembered her manners then. "I'm sorry, sir. Please sir, where is the law? Where will I find the constable?"

He jerked a thumb and said crossly, "The young 'uns are getting ruder every day. Like to knock me off my feet. Over there."

She darted into the open door he indicated. Two men were standing by the barred window. One gave her a pleasant nod and the other frowned, and their conversation went on. She waited politely, trying to think what to say when there was a break in the talking. She looked at the empty cell at the back of the room, at the heavy bars on the door. But she couldn't wait forever, just looking.

"Sir?" she said timidly, not sure which one to address. "Sir?"

"Later, child," said the frowner. "I tell you, I demand satisfaction and I won't leave Pittsburgh until I get it. I can't say that the law is giving me much support."

"Can't get blood out of a turnip," replied the other. "This is a big town and I've got more to do than — "

"Sir?" said Serena again, and this time the man turned and looked at her. "Please," she said, "we've got a couple of robbers tied up on our raft, and my pa'd be much obliged if you would come and get them. They're the Brownsville robbers."

"On your raft? Where is your raft?"

"We're tied up right near here. I'll show you. It's the boat-store raft."

"Raft!" shouted the long-faced man. "Boat-store raft? That may be the one my nephew's on!"

"Take it easy, Mr. Bunby. We'll get the robbers first and hunt your nephew later." He grabbed his gun from the wall and started out the door. Serena stood rooted to the floor. This must be John's Uncle Matthew, and she had spilled the beans.

"Wait," said Mr. Bunby. "Wait, girl! Is there a young fellow traveling on your raft, tall, fair-skinned, name of John Bunby?"

Serena knew what Ma and Pa thought about lying, but this seemed to her more like bamboozlement. "No," she said, "no, no, no!" and she raced to keep up with the constable.

John wasn't fair-skinned any longer. He was sunburned as red as an Indian, and his real name was John Fenton. "No," she called over her shoulder, "nobody by that name."

She had to beat the constable and Mr. Bunby, had to get to the raft in time to warn John that his uncle was coming. Desperation made her feet fly. The heavy-footed officer of the law was well behind when she clambered down the ladder and thumped onto the raft.

"Hide, John!" she squeaked. She was so out of breath

she could hardly gasp out the words. "Your uncle — "

John clenched his fist. "I'll not let him stop me!"

"No punchin'," said Pa. "Into the shanty, quick. We'll handle this with bamboozlement if we can. Hurry!"

By the time the constable had located the boat-store and climbed down the ladder John was out of sight. The Dowell family stood around their two trussed robbers, smiling broadly.

"The Brownsville robbers," said Pa, shaking hands. "We're mighty glad to get rid of them. Stand 'em up, Luke."

"The Brownsville robbers? You got proof?" asked the constable.

Pa thought a moment.

"You got to have proof," insisted the constable. "What makes you think they're the ones? How do I know — "

"We've got the proof," said a voice from the shanty.

"No, John," said Pa, but the door opened anyway. John came out, holding the ledger in which he had sketched the robbers.

"Can't be helped, Mr. Dowell," he said. "We've got to make sure Gus and Lorenzo don't get away scot-free."

He told the constable his story and showed him the drawings in the ledger.

Gustus and Lorenzo groaned and rolled their eyes and looked at John as if they would like to throttle him, but the stockings stuffed in their mouths silenced their words.

"Good thing they can't speak what they're thinkin'," Ma whispered to Serena. "Wouldn't be fittin' for our ears."

The constable was convinced as soon as he got a look at the pictures.

"Well done," he said. "These 'uns'll end up in jail for sure. I gather there's a sizable reward in it for you folks, offered by the gent who was robbed. Why, look here, here he comes now. Dagnab it, why won't he let me alone?"

Newtie was there too. He shouted, "We got a customer, Pa! I was lost but I got found again, and I showed this fellow the way!"

They all looked up at the wharf above them. Newtie and the stranger looked down. Newtie was smiling but the stranger was not. He was a long-faced man with a sour expression, the same man Serena had seen in the constable's office.

"Oh, Newtie," she whispered. "You've done it this time."

"Not a very cheerful cuss," Pa said, under his breath. "With a long face like that, he could eat oats out of a butter churn. Reach right down to the bottom."

John's Uncle Matthew climbed down the ladder and stepped out on the raft.

"Well, nephew," he said. "Did you think I wouldn't find you? Get your things. We're starting back to Brownsville."

"No!" said John. "Not that. I'm on my way, and you can't stop me."

Mr. Bunby turned to the constable. "Do your job, officer. Handcuff him if necessary. This runaway boy will return with me."

"If he does, it will have to be of his own free will," said the constable. "I've got more things to do than chase down every runaway that passes through Pittsburgh. You found him, now you persuade him. Here's some genuine lawbreakers I've got to attend to. Why, they're said to be the very ones who robbed you! Take a look, Mr. Bunby. Are they the ones who skinned you?"

Mr. Bunby noticed the tied-up pair for the first time. His eyes bugged out.

"Those're two of them," he shouted. "I'd recognize that scar anywhere — and the other one too. Good work, constable. I'm glad you stirred yourself to do your duty at last."

"They were caught purely by the gumption of your nephew, no one else," Pa put in quickly. "You have him to thank."

"And where's the money? Where's all my hard-earned money? And where's the third fellow?"

Pa scratched his head. "We don't rightly know the answers to those questions, but like as not the constable'll have ways of findin' out."

John said, "We've got an idea. We've been thinking maybe the third fellow might really be a woman. Whichever, the third one must be the one who's got the valise full of money. The start he or she's got, maybe coming downstream on the steamboat, that third one could be a hundred miles away by now."

Lorenzo started to sputter then. His face grew red and he glared angrily at Gustus.

"Seems like that idea riles him up a mite," observed the constable. "I'll have to have a little talk with him about this. Here, boys," he said to Luke and John, "help me tie them together so they can't get away, and then we'll loosen up their leg ropes enough so they can shuffle up the ladder. Don't fancy lifting them up deadweight if I can help it."

It took only a moment to lash Gustus and Lorenzo together and add a lead line for the constable to hang onto. They could move their legs enough to climb clumsily up the ladder but they were too hobbled to run away. The Dowells all watched as the constable half boosted, half dragged them onto the wharf and then set them going at a mincing trot.

"It'll be a long time before Lorenzo forgets this day," said Ma. "Serves him right, speakin' harshly to Sweet Harmony."

The constable and his charges were well on their way when Ma remembered the stockings. "Dagnab it, there's a perfectly good pair of warm stockings gone. A lot of knittin' time went into them. Later on, Serena, we'll call on the constable and get 'em back."

"I can show you the way, Ma," Serena said smugly. "I didn't get lost."

Newtie was ruffled. "Aw, Serena, I wasn't lost for long. And how was I to know — "

"Good thing you did show Mr. Bunby the way, Newtie," said Pa. "Can't say I was so glad to see him at first, but now I think there's some matters that have to be talked about."

"There's nothing to talk about," said John and his uncle together.

"Pair of hardheads if I ever saw 'em," said Pa. "But, by ginger, let's sit down anyway. We'll jaw at it a bit and see if we can't come up with an answer."

11

Pa Wins Out

THERE'S ONLY ONE answer. You'll get your things, John Bunby, and come with me. We're taking the next steamer upriver to Brownsville. I've wasted enough time on this matter."

"Not so fast, Mr. Bunby. Aren't you even curious about what made John decide to leave? I think you owe John a chance to explain what he aims to do with his life."

Mr. Bunby sputtered. "What he aims to do? It's what I aim for him to do!"

Pa insisted, "It's his future, by ginger, and you owe him a chance to talk about it."

"Owe? Poppycock! I am grateful to you for returning my nephew to my custody, and I owe you some thanks. I owe you a reward for catching the thieves, and you'll

get it. I am a man of my word. Other than that I owe nothing to anyone."

"You're not listenin'!" said Pa. "You're a stubborn, mule-headed old alligator!"

"There's nothing more to be said. Get your belongings, John."

"Why you low-down, hang-jawed, weasel-eyed — " Pa began. His face was red under its sun-brown, and Mr. Bunby's face was almost purple, as if his neckcloth were choking him.

"You, sir, are nothing but a mud-born river roller!" Pa clenched his fists. For a moment it looked as if there was going to be a fight. Mr. Bunby towered over Pa but he didn't look as if he'd ever done much scrapping. He backed up a step as Pa advanced on him.

Then Pa lowered his fists and began to grin. He held out his hand instead. "Mr. Bunby, we're neither of us ring-tailed roarers, settlin' our dispute with punchin'. We're just two men who want to see this boy done right by, each accordin' to his own lights. There's more'n one way of gettin' out of a skunk hole. It's up to us to find the way."

Mr. Bunby finally shook Pa's hand. What else could he do with Pa smiling so cheerfully and wanting to be friends?

"Sit down," said Pa. "We can all work on this thing."

Unwillingly, Mr. Bunby seated himself on a haybag. John sat down too, just as unwillingly. He did not look at his uncle.

It was easy to tell that Mr. Bunby did not feel comfortable. He sat bolt upright with his legs sticking out in front of him. His long face was more sour than ever, Serena thought, as he looked anywhere but at John.

Pa lounged between the two, leaning back against the shanty wall. He had not said this was to be a private conference, so Ma had quickly settled herself on the other haybag. Serena did not intend to be left out, and neither did Luke and Newtie, unless Pa signaled that they were to leave. They stood very still, trying not to call any attention to themselves. Only Sweet Harmony was unconcerned. She squatted nearby, fascinated by a bug that was making its way up and down the hilly route across the logs.

"Now," said Pa, just when it seemed as if the uneasy silence was going to last forever, "there's a few things we should lay out on the table, so to speak. Have to arrive at some understanding. Now, John, here's your chance. You explain yourself to your uncle plain and clear. Tell him what you've got on your mind."

It took John a moment to get going, but once he started it all came tumbling out: his unhappiness at the bank, at the career that had been forced on him, and his desperate need to be an artist like his father — even better, maybe, if he could get the proper training. He told how he meant to make his way to Philadelphia by stagecoach and find a painter there who'd take him on and teach him.

"I know I'll have to work hard. There's nothing easy about it, even if it does seem to come natural to me. I have to try, and I'll never make it if I go on working as a clerk in your office. I've tried, honest I have, and every day I work there is like being in prison. I've got to be an artist!"

Uncle Matthew grunted scornfully. "An artist! A shiftless roamer with no home and no goods except what you can carry in a wagon!"

He had more to say on this point, but Ma burst out, "And what's wrong with that, I'd like to know? Right now, us Dowells have no home and no goods except for what you see right on this raft, but we're a long way from bein' shiftless roamers! Dagnab it, we're a family, and a good family, and where we happen to make our home has nothin' to do with it!"

In spite of the seriousness of the situation, Pa grinned. "Never thought I'd hear you say that, Lucinda."

"Well, it's true, Henry! And Mr. Bunby here had better understand it. This boy may have had a fancy Bunby roof over his head, but he hasn't had a real family!"

Mr. Bunby wasn't convinced. He wasn't even listening. He went on, "Don't you see, nephew, I rescued you from just that sort of no-account life. I'm offering you a chance to be a somebody, a chance at a respectable position, maybe considerable wealth someday if you apply yourself, and you don't seem to appreciate it. What kind of foolish talk is this? You'll find it's only a weakness that you'll get over if you make the effort."

John bristled, but Pa held up his hand.

"Now, Mr. Bunby, bein' no-account has nothing to do with it. I've heard tell of artist fellows who do right well at takin' off likenesses and such. Have themselves houses and carriages, all the worldly goods you set such store by. And come to think of it, I've heard of bankers who had shiftless streaks or downright mean streaks, for that matter. The thing is, this paintin' and drawin' is what makes the sun rise and set for the boy. He's got a gift, you can't deny that."

"If you can call it that."

Pa rushed on before Mr. Bunby could say anything more. "If a man finds his guidin' star when he's young enough to follow where it leads, I think that's a pure wonderment. To work hard and make your living at the thing that pleasures you most, that's a gracious plenty. It's all a man could ask from life. It's true happiness."

Serena felt a lump in her throat. There was a sad note in Pa's voice that seemed to grab at her.

"You've found your way, Mr. Bunby. Why take away John's chance to do the same?"

Pa's earnest appeal seemed to melt Mr. Bunby a little.

"Well," he said to John uncertainly, "your Aunt Julia and I — it's a great responsibility — we only want to do what's best — "

"Let me try it for a year," begged John. "Test me out, see how I do. If it's just a weakness, as you say, I'll know in that time."

Ma said quickly, "He's a good boy, Mr. Bunby, with a good head on his shoulders. You'll see."

Mr. Bunby found himself swept along. Finally he nodded, persuaded in spite of himself. "A year," he said. "No more'n a year to try it out. By that time I warrant you'll be glad to come home to Brownsville with your tail between your legs."

"As for the reward," said Pa, striking while the iron was hot, "we'd never've caught those varmints if it hadn't been for your nephew's drawings. So if you do get your money back, John could use the reward to help him get started in Philadelphia. Agreed?"

Mr. Bunby nodded again. He wasn't much of a man for smiling. His face was as sour as ever, but there was a kinder tone in his voice.

"All right, John. You're to have your chance, it seems. If you change your mind before the steamboat leaves in the morning, you'll find me at the Hotel Paradise."

"Paradise?" asked Ma and John together. "Paradise! Of course, the *Hotel* Paradise! That's what they meant!"

Mr. Bunby and Pa stared, but Serena caught on right away. Ma was so excited she was screeching.

"John, go straight there! Stay by the door so's you'll see her — or him — if she tries to leave! Serena, you know the way. Find the constable and tell him to hurry!"

John was halfway up the ladder when he turned to shout, "I don't know where the hotel is! Come on, Uncle Matthew, you'll have to show me!"

Mr. Bunby didn't wait for an explanation. He hurried after his nephew. As she watched them dash though the crowds ahead of her, Serena thought, I'll bet that's the first time those two ever did anything together.

*

They had a lot of explaining to do that evening, Serena and Luke and Newtie. The boys had raced after her in the rush to find the constable. Newtie was determined not to get lost this time, and Luke wasn't going to be left out either. But it was Serena who knew exactly where to find the constable's office. And it was Serena who understood the importance of the Hotel Paradise. The boys could only stand back and listen as Serena gasped out to the constable, "The robbers were planning to meet at the Hotel Paradise. Maybe the third one's there, the one with the money! And maybe it's a woman! Hurry!"

The constable might have waited for more of an explanation, but a loud groan from the cell behind him made it clear that Serena was on the right track.

"I told you!" cried Lorenzo. "I told you not to let her go with all the money — "

Gustus clapped a hand over his mouth but Lorenzo had already said more than enough.

"Come on!" said the constable. In a flash he had grabbed his gun, locked the door, and was off down the street with the three Dowells behind him.

"And that was it," said Serena as they all sat on the raft eating their supper. "The lady robber was there, all right. She was all dressed up, packed and ready to go. She had just about decided to run off and leave Gustus and Lorenzo, figuring they weren't going to make it. Caught her red-handed."

"And," said Luke, "Mr. Bunby's money was jammed into a valise under the bed. He got most of it back, except for her steamboat fare and the hotel bill."

[113]

"He was so happy he almost smiled," reported Newtie. "Not quite — it would've split his face open — but almost."

"I reckon there's good in the man," Pa said, "but it's buried powerful deep."

"Well, now." Ma took a deep breath. "That's that. It'll be strange goin' on without John. Seems like he made a place for himself in our family in a mighty short time. He'll leave a hole where he used to be." She sighed. "He's a big boy, but he's only a boy. Fourteen's awful young to be in a big city, makin' his way all alone. I'm glad it's not you goin', Luke."

"Me, too," said Luke. "I like it where I am."

"And where we are is right here, all of us together. But John's story is turnin' out well, thanks to you, Henry. That was a mighty fine speech you made. It swept Mr. Bunby right off his feet."

"Pure bamboozlement, Lucinda."

"Not entirely, Henry. Sounded to me like it came straight from the heart," Ma answered. "Gave me somethin' to ponder on."

12

The Storm

HE DOWELLS MADE a quick trip ashore the next morning just to look at the bustling city. This time Ma and Harmony stayed behind. Ma said Brownsville was as big a town as she cared to think about, and even that had turned out to be more exciting than she'd bargained for.

They were all back at the raft again, getting ready to shove off, when they saw John hurrying out on the wharf.

"The stage for Philadelphia leaves soon," he panted, "but I wanted to say good-by. And to thank you, more than I can say. I'll be thinking about you all, finding your farm, building your new house. Will you write to me someday, care of my uncle? I'd like to let you know how I make out."

They promised, and Ma hugged him good-by, and then he was off again. They waved and waved until he was out of sight.

"Well," said Pa, "nothing to do now but cast off. Untie the ropes, boys. I'll take her out into the current. We're on our way."

"On our way to our farm," said Ma. "When we get past the city and into the Ohio River we can start lookin' for a likely place. Seems like all the world is movin' down the Ohio — there go two more rafts like ours. You can bet they'll be lookin', too. We should hurry. There's still time to get in a late crop if we don't dally."

They did dally, though. It was impossible to float past likely-looking settlements when the folks ran right down to the landing and urged Pa to tie up the Floating Emporium and do business.

"What can I do?" asked Pa. "Lucinda, they're a-beggin' us to stop. They need what we've got."

"Oh well," Ma agreed, "It'll give us a chance to pasture Lilybelle for a while, and I can look around for land while you're tradin'."

Ma was hard to please. "Too hilly," she'd say. "Too stony. We'd spend all our days pickin' out rocks." Or, "Too far from anywhere. We ought to find a place near a settlement, so's the children can get some schoolin'. Don't want 'em to grow up ignorant."

"Suits me all right," said Newtie, and reached for the rifle. "I'll get us some squirrels for stew while Serena picks greens. Don't need schoolin' for that."

"Nevertheless," Ma insisted, "we need a good spring,

[116]

and rich level land, and we won't settle for less."

At each stop it seemed to Serena that Pa took longer to make his trades. It took him longer afterward to put the shelves in order. There was something sad about the way he smoothed out every wrinkle in the calico before he rolled up the bolts again.

"I'll have to admit it, Lucinda," he said. "I'll miss the store. This spell of storekeepin' has been a pure pleasurement, every day of it." He added hastily, "That's not to say that I'm not lookin' forward to our new farm, but . . ."

"I can get in a state just thinkin' about it," said Ma. "We'll be sleepin' like royalty on our new beds. I declare, Henry, you've traded for a nice lot of feathers, enough to make feather ticks for us all, bags and bags full."

Pa looked up at the sky. "There was a ring around the moon three nights ago, and a mackerel sky yesterday. We'd better get those feathers under cover in the shanty. I'm afeard we're due for a pour-down by the looks of things."

They all worked to shift things around and make room in the shanty. Luke and Newtie lugged in the big sacks of feathers and Ma stuffed them into what little space they could make. The air was damp and chilly, and for the first time in weeks the sun didn't shine.

"High time we got rain," Luke said. "It'll help the pasture. I notice the fields around here are mighty dry and dusty, and the corn's not doing much. Little bits of straggly shoots."

[117]

"It's good country, just the same," said Ma. "Just a mite short of rain this spring, that's all, and it looks as if that's goin' to change. Serena, tend to the hens. I'm goin' to make a batch of johnnycake afore it gets too wet to keep the fire goin'."

The hens had been scratching around on the roof and did not take kindly to being shut up in their pen. But Serena herded them inside and made sure they had enough food and fresh water. The broody hen was still sitting on the duck eggs.

"How long before these hatch, Ma?" Serena called.

"I've lost track of the days. Anytime now, I'd guess. Takes about three weeks from layin' to hatchin'. Cover old Broody up well, and don't disturb her."

The johnnycake was done just in time. The first drops of rain began to sizzle on the hot stove top before they had quite finished mopping up their squirrel stew.

They had had a few brief showers from time to time, the kind that came on fast and hard and dried up almost as quickly. They had run into not one soaking day-long rain on all their trip, nothing that made them eat or sleep inside the shanty. This rain looked as if it planned to stay around for a spell.

Serena put her shawl over her head and sat outside for a while. At first the rain only dimpled the river; then, driven by the wind, it blew across in misty sheets. Finally Ma called her inside, and she left Pa and the boys to steer and watch for snags.

They tied up early that night. It was cold johnnycake

and the leftover stew for supper. Nobody minded too much. But the next morning it was raining harder than ever. The shanty roof was leaking in a dozen places, and a hot breakfast would have been mighty tasty in all the dampness.

They all struggled together to lash a big tarpaulin over the roof and tie it down. It kept some of the rain out, all right, but the shanty was dark and airless, and they were very conscious of the chicken coop right overhead.

"Smells like the bottom of a skunk hole in here," complained Ma. "And I can't see my hand before my face." She tried to wedge the shanty door open a trifle, but the wind caught it. The door slammed open and shut with such force that they had to tie it closed. After that it was darker and smellier than ever.

For a long time they had drifted along in sunshine. The river had been smooth, riffled here and there as it swirled around rocks or fallen trees. Steering had been easy. Traveling by raft was lazy going.

Now, quite suddenly, things had changed. Pa hung onto the sweep and yelled to Luke and Newtie, "Keep your eyes peeled for snags! Give me warnin' so's I can steer out in time. Look out for that low branch! By ginger, that was a close call!"

As one little swollen creek after another tumbled into the Ohio, the going got rougher. Finally Pa said, "Keep watchin', Newtie. Luke, you give me a hand here and we'll turn her in to shore. We'll have to tie up until this blasted storm blows itself out."

[119]

Even with two heaving on the sweep, Pa had a time edging the raft out of the swirling current. And when he did run them aground, it was with a crunching crash that jarred their teeth.

"Sorry about this, Lucinda," Pa apologized. "We'll lose a day's good travelin' and lookin' time."

"Can't be helped," said Ma. "Take off those wet clothes and get warm before you all catch your death."

The shanty was crowded with all of them inside. There was no room to move around without crawling over somebody's feet. They remembered Lorenzo's feet and giggled, but after a while it wasn't funny anymore. They began to be cross and cranky.

"None of that," Pa said. "It's too tight a fit in here for temper. Let's have some music."

Ma fixed a box bed for Harmony and hung it on ropes from the ceiling. The novelty of a bed swinging above everybody's heads amused the little girl. She laughed and clapped in time to Pa's mouth organ.

Pa played until he was out of puff, and then he got them all to singing until they ran out of songs. Then he told all the jokes he could remember, and made up a few new ones. Ma remembered stories of how it had been when she was a little girl. They imagined how it must be with John, on his way to Philadelphia — how he would find a place to stay and an artist to work with.

Ma worried. "I hope John is out of this pour-down. He's got nobody to make him change into dry clothes."

They talked about Philadelphia, what a big city it was.

Bigger even than Pittsburgh, Pa said, although Serena found that hard to believe. Nothing could be bigger than Pittsburgh.

And after all that it was still only midday.

"Confuse and confound!" said Ma. "I never did know a day to go by so slow."

Sweet Harmony was hungry and said so, loud and clear. The third time she said it, Ma sighed and said, "Nothin' but a little johnnycake. You can have it with honey or molasses for sweetener — that is, provided I can find the honey in the dark."

The long, dull afternoon finally passed. No one was very hungry for more cornbread, and after supper they all turned in.

Pa checked the animals and the ropes once more before he went to bed. "It's blowin' for fair!" he gasped when he had struggled inside again. "We'll have another few hours of this, I reckon, before we can start out again."

"Long as we're tied up safe and all together, we'll weather it," said Ma. "When the pour-down's ended we can start lookin' for farmland again. I can pass the time happy just thinkin' about the lovely farm we're goin' to find soon."

Serena went to sleep with the sound of the rain beating on the tarpaulin. Sometime during the night the wind rose to a howl. The river was lashed to a heaving boil. The raft strained against the ropes, and suddenly one gave way. The raft swung wildly, and the other rope

parted. The Floating Emporium was loose. Out of control, on its way down the Ohio River.

Inside the shanty, the lurch and heave tumbled the family all together, frightened out of sleep, confused. Harmony fell from her swinging bed and cried. The Dowells could hang on only to one another.

Pa struggled to his knees. He shouted over the noise of the storm, "Got to get out there! Maybe if I steered — " but Ma held on to him.

"No!" she yelled. "You'd be washed over!"

A splintering crash interrupted her. The raft struck something but swept on. In another second there was a snap, sharp as a rifle shot, and Pa groaned.

"That must've been the sweep. Broke clean off. We haven't got a chance now. Oh, Lucinda." His voice broke. "I brought it on you all by my swappin' and tradin'!"

Ma's voice was shaking too. "Twaddle!" she said. "It wasn't anybody's fault. We won't seek blame tinder. We'll wait our way out of this. Pray and wait and sing."

They did just that. They sang every song they had ever heard, over and over. Even Sweet Harmony joined in. Pa had to laugh.

"It took a storm to mellow our Sweet Harmony. We can hope her mood lasts when the sun comes out — if it ever does." He had to yell to be heard over the shriek of the wind and the groaning of the timbers under them.

It might have been days that they huddled there in the dark, but most likely it only felt that long. The raft swung and tilted under them. Then there was a splintering, jarring crash that tumbled them all in a heap. The raft was swept up at a crazy slant. They braced themselves for a steep tilt in the opposite direction — and nothing happened. The Floating Emporium had come to a sudden stop.

13

Shipwrecked

T WAS A long time before anyone could speak.

"Wha-what happened?" Serena finally asked.

Pa picked himself up. "Blamed if I know," he said. "We're stuck on something. If we're lucky we'll hang here until the storm is over. Then we can figure out what to do. I guess we'd better try to sleep now, if we can."

Sweet Harmony finally dropped off, but that was only because she was too young to know what was going on. The rest lay still, staring into the darkness, not daring to move for fear the slightest shift might cause the raft to come unstuck.

Once Ma whispered, "The wind's dying down, don't you think? Doesn't seem so loud."

Maybe it was, but Serena couldn't tell for sure. The

roar of the water drowned out every other sound.

Poor Lilybelle had long since stopped her frantic mooing, scared silent. On the other side of the shanty wall there was an occasional tired squeal from the pigs. If the hens hadn't been drowned, it would be a pure wonderment. And the little ducks inside the eggs, what about them?

At last there was no doubt. The storm was over.

Pa crawled over Luke and Newtie to the door. "Everybody sit tight," he ordered. "Don't lash around until I see how we're fixed."

He struggled up the slope, untied the door, and peered outside. Turning back, he explained. "We're jammed up on a big fallen tree. Looks like we're secure enough if we don't rassle around. And if we're careful, soon's the river goes down a bit we can walk ashore on the tree trunk and never even get our feet wet. By dabs, Lucinda, we've done it again!"

"You do have a knack for landin' us right side up," said Ma. "You've even bamboozled the river."

"Nothing I did. Pure dumb luck, but I'm grateful for it."

That was a long day, but not nearly as long as the day that went before. They could brace the shanty door open and get some light and fresh air.

Pa was firm about not rassling around.

"If we get bumped loose now, the raft'll break apart and we'll lose everything. Be patient, sit tight, and the river'll start goin' down. In a few hours we can unload and begin to dry out."

It wasn't easy to be patient. They were all wet through, and by now they were hungry. Serena had never in her life been so hungry. If she could get out and run around, get busy at something, maybe it would take her mind off the huge growling cavity that was her stomach. But there was not one thing she could do but lie very still and think.

Serene, she said to herself. Now's the time for me to be easy and serene, like Pa said, and wait for things to happen. The idea didn't appeal to her at all. I'll never be able to do it, she decided. I'll never be able to live up to my name, no matter what Pa says. Ma's a get-up-and-doer, and so's Pa in his own way. And I'm a mixture of them both — a hungry mixture, to boot.

Another fearful growl from her stomach interrupted her thoughts and made her laugh.

The cornbread was gone, but Ma pawed around in the clutter and found the molasses keg. She poured them each a spoonful. It was the best she could do, and it did help to take away their ravenous appetites.

"If we could just get 'em tuned, we could have us a little orchestra just with the rumblin' of our stomachs," said Pa.

Serena giggled. Even being hungry wasn't so bad when you could make a joke of it. And she could sit there on her soggy haybag and think about the dinner they'd cook once they got ashore and had a good fire going.

Pa ventured out to see to the animals, inching his way along the uptilted raft. "I'm afraid if I so much as sneeze,

I'll jar us loose," he reported. "We're hanging on by the grace of God and a couple of branches. But the river's goin' down. Already I can see the difference."

Finally he said, "I think we dare chance it, Lucinda. Now, now," he added as a cheer went up, "go easy there! We aren't out of this yet. I'll go first and see what's what, and then I'll be back to help you off one by one."

Serena held her breath as Pa wobbled across the fallen tree, hanging onto the branches and picking his way with care. He scrambled up the bank and disappeared. In a few minutes he was back again.

"By ginger and jiminy, we're in luck again. If we had to be shipwrecked, we picked the right place for it. There's a fine little meadow nearby, high enough above the river to be safe even if it rains some more. Come on, but come carefully."

"Oh my mercy, I'll be glad to get my feet back on dry land again," said Ma.

Ma's dry land wasn't very dry, and neither were their feet. But it felt wonderful to be walking around on any kind of land at all. One by one they walked across the tree-trunk bridge and climbed the muddy bank. There was a barrier of brush and then the meadow.

The sun was struggling to come through the clouds. It was a pale, watery sun, but there was some warmth to it, and a promise of drier times to come.

Pa sorted through the tools and found a couple of hatchets, and he and the boys hacked off the branches that made the bridge hard to cross, leaving only enough for handholds here and there. Then they cut a path through the brush and they were ready to start unloading.

"We'll take everything off the raft and see what we can rescue," said Pa. "The goods must be soaked through. Water won't hurt most of it, though. We'll just dump out the nail kegs and wipe off the tools. The buttons and such'll dry off fine as can be."

"Whatever got wet will get dry," said Ma. "Just as we will. First though, we've got to do what we can for those poor critters. Lilybelle must have been scared out of her wits. She'll welcome this nice meadow grass."

Lilybelle protested, but Luke and Serena patted and soothed and coaxed her down the sloping raft, into water up to her belly, and up the bank. They tied her on a long tether so she could graze wherever she cared to.

"Go up and see what's happened to the hens, Serena," said Ma.

"Half-drowned," Serena reported from the roof, "but they're all here in the coop. And Ma, Ma, the duck eggs hatched!"

Two of the newly hatched ducklings had not made it through the storm, but two were huddled under the old broody hen, alive and warm.

"It's like a miracle," breathed Serena. "All that wind and rain, and them so little."

"It's a fine beginning for our new farm," said Ma, her face all shiny and bright with pleasure. "It's a sign that things are going to go well."

Together Ma and Serena wrestled the hen coop up to

the meadow. The hens squawked faintly and ruffled their wet feathers and then sat, dull-eyed and miserable.

"Poor things," said Ma. "They'd dry better if they could move around. Newtie and Serena, help me put together a pen."

It was a crude little chicken yard that they made in a hurry, just branches stuck in the ground close together with other twigs woven in and out. It wouldn't do for long, but until the hens were feeling friskier it would be fine. In one corner of the pen Serena and Ma scratched together a dry nest for the broody hen and the two little ducklings.

"There you are," said Ma. "You peck up a nice mess of worms and you'll soon feel at home."

The two pigs were something else again. They lay against the shanty and refused to move.

"Ain't nothin' as independent as a hog," said Pa, scratching his head. "They won't listen to coaxin' nor jollyin'. They just won't move."

"When they do decide to take off, they'll run for miles," said Ma. "We need a pen for them too, but it can't be just twigs and leaves."

"Lilybelle's stall," suggested Luke. "We can knock that apart and get it built again strong enough to hold the porkers."

Pa and the boys pried the nails out of the logs and soon had the stall all apart. Pa stood looking at the raft.

"Makes me feel sorta bad to see the old Emporium comin' apart like this."

[131]

"Can't be helped, Pa," said Newtie sensibly. "That was the way we planned it back on the Monongahela."

"I know," Pa took up his ax again and tried to smile. "It's the way things have to be. The adventure's over. We never expected it to go on forever."

Serena gulped and grabbed her end of the log rail. It gave her a funny hurting feeling to see Pa so down in the mouth, all the ginger and jiminy gone out of his talk. There was no time to think about it, though. Newtie started up the bank and Serena had to scramble to keep up.

A shout from the river stopped them in their tracks just as they reached the top. "Hey! Hey, there! Boat-store, you got any grub for sale?"

A flatboat loaded with logs was going by, moving fast on the still turbulent river. The steersman called again, "Any grub for sale?"

Pa shook his head and shouted, "Nothing for sale! We're shipwrecked!"

Back before the storm hit Ma and Pa had talked things over. They had decided not to sell any more.

"We're gettin' low on things," Ma had said. "We'll need all we've got left to get our own house built and the new farm started."

And Pa had agreed. "We're almost to the bottom on some things. You're right, Lucinda. We just won't make any more sales."

So now he shouted to the boatman, "Sorry, nothing for sale!" The boat was soon out of sight around the bend.

In a few minutes a raft came into view, closer to the shore and moving more slowly.

"A store!" someone yelled. "Look, a store! What have you got?"

"Nothing for sale," Pa shouted again. "We're out of business!"

"Too bad," said the man at the sweep. His wife waved her apron and a big dog ran to the edge of the raft and barked.

"It is too bad," said Pa after they were gone. "It doesn't seem right to let a sure-enough customer get away. Oh, well — grab aholt here, Luke, and we'll get these logs up to the meadow in no time."

Ma had a good fire going. The kettle was boiling and something smelled good.

"Water didn't hurt the bacon," she said. "Just washed some of the salt out of it. And wet cornmeal is as good as dry when you're makin' mush. Sit down, all of you, and eat hearty. We've been a long time without a good hot meal."

Serena thought that bacon and mush had never tasted so good. And sunshine and a warm breeze had never been so welcome.

Pa was silent for a long time, for him. Finally he said, "Lucinda, is this the place? Is this the land you've been lookin' for?"

"It's level," she said. "And high enough above the river to be safe from flooding."

"The soil seems rich," said Pa. "Sweet Harmony here is our muddy-faced proof that the dirt's good and dark."

He shifted the little girl to his other knee and speared another piece of bacon from the skillet.

"I've been thinkin'. Before we put the pen up and get the pigs ashore, I should scout around and see if there's any sign of another farmer on this piece of land. Could be, you know. Could be someone just beyond the woods there. I'll check it out if this place pleases you."

"It'll do just fine," said Ma. "Time we settled down after all our traipsin' and got a crop in."

"Then I'll get movin'. I'll be back afore long, Lucinda. We'll soon know if this'll be our new home."

"I wish you were as pleased as I am, Henry," said Ma. "I wish you were as eager to be rooted in one place."

"I knew it had to come to an end sometime, honey, the sellin' and tradin' and bamboozlin'. Couldn't last forever. No, I'm pleased, too."

They all watched as Pa walked through the meadow grass to the woods.

"Your pa ain't steppin' very high," Ma said. "Seems like some of the starch has gone out of him."

14

Two Stars to Follow

SERENA SWALLOWED HARD. "Ma, would it be so bad? I mean to be storekeepers? Pa is so clever at tradin' and sellin' — "

"I know. It plain breaks my heart to spoil his pleasure. When he made that speech to Mr. Bunby, it gave me a lot to think about. 'A man should follow his star,' he said, and I know what he was thinkin'."

She stared at the trees where Pa had disappeared.

"But a storekeeper has to go *to* people, unless he's in a town. He has to go with a wagon or a pack on his back, or a raft, to wherever folks are. And a raft's no place to raise a family. We're not roamers, Serena. We need land and a settled place for you young 'uns. I've tried to think otherwise. I've turned it every which way in my mind, and there's no other answer. We're farmers. We have to have a farm."

Serena knew Ma was right, but it was sad just the same.

Ma sighed. Then she said briskly, "Well, now, no call to stand around. There's plenty to do to keep busy until your pa gets back."

They fluffed the bags of damp feathers and tossed the hay from the haybags in the sunshine. They stirred the cornmeal that was spread out to dry in every available container.

Newtie played horsie with Sweet Harmony to tire her out so she would take a nap. It was Newtie who finally collapsed in a heap.

"I'm the one who needs the nap," he panted. "Look at her — she's all ready to go around the meadow again and I'm wore out."

Ma took mercy on him.

"I'll sit here and hold her for a spell," she said. "You all pick greens for the pigs. Whatever news Pa brings, they'll be stuck on the raft at least until tomorrow. Feed the poor things well."

"Seems like pigs don't care one way or another," said Newtie as they tossed in armloads of grass. "They don't care if we settle here or have to move on, long as we give them enough to eat."

The pigs were grunting happily and noisily, and at first the Dowells didn't hear the shout. "Halloo!" it came again.

A big raft was coming in closer, a man at the sweep

and a woman with a pole pushing as hard as she could against the current.

"Oh, please, we saw your sign — have you any corn-meal?" the woman called.

Luke answered. "We aren't a store anymore. We got shipwrecked in the storm. We've only enough left to carry us."

"Oh, Lordy!" The couple had shoved the raft out of the current and could rest a minute. "We're right out. Our meal barrel broke loose and washed overboard."

Two shy children peered out from the safety of the shanty. The roof over them was almost open to the sky.

"Hit us bad, the storm did," the man said. "Hardly any supplies left."

"Wait," said Serena. "I'll ask Ma."

She scrambled up the bank and raced back to the meadow. "Ma," she said, whispering because Sweet Harmony had finally dropped off to sleep. "There's a family on a raft with two little ones and no cornmeal. They lost it all in the storm. Can we sell them just a little?"

Ma wrinkled her forehead. "We agreed we wouldn't sell a thing more. We want to keep all we've got to carry us through until we get in a crop. Two little ones, did you say? And not a bit of meal?"

"Not much of anything, seems like."

It didn't take Ma long to decide.

"We won't sell it to them. Things have gone well for us this summer. We can pass on a little of our good luck. Grab aholt here, Serena. We can let them have this

[137]

bucketful as a present."

She gave a quick look at Sweet Harmony, sprawled out on a blanket in the shade.

"She's out for a good while. We'll just carry this down to them. Careful now, don't spill it. It'd be sinful to waste a speck."

"I — we — I don't know how to say thank you." The woman choked. "We've got a bit of jerked beef and some sweetening, and now we'll have mush and bread. Oh, we'll be just fine now."

"Settlin' hereabouts?" Ma asked.

"No, we're planning to go farther down the river — " the man began, but his wife said swiftly, "Yes! Here-abouts! You promised me we'd be no farther than a day's journey from a store, like we were back home. And here we are with a real store. Yes! We're going to find us some land nearby! Neighbors and a store! I never dreamed we'd be so lucky."

The current caught them, and the shaky raft started on its way.

"Good-by, and thank you," they called. "We'll be back to trade as soon as we make our first crop."

"Well," said Ma when they were out of sight. "Well! That was a surprise. Neighbors, already."

An idea was buzzing around in Serena's head. She tried to pin it down and say what was on her mind.

"Ma, couldn't there be two stars?"

Ma stared at her.

"Stars? It's broad daylight, child."

"No, no. I mean, couldn't we follow two stars? A farm star for you and a trading star for Pa? You heard what that lady said, they'd be back and they would come to *us*, she said. People could come to us, to Pa's store, and we could stay right here. Oh Ma, couldn't we have it both ways?"

Ma sat down with a thump. "I never thought of it except as all one way or the other. Maybe . . ."

Luke remembered the boats from the morning. "There'll be more of them, Ma. This river'll be full of flatboats and keelboats and rafts."

"Even steamboats," added Newtie. "Steamboats all need wood to fire up their boilers. We can sell 'em wood."

"And Pa said this country would be filling up fast. Folks'll need all sorts of things to start their farms, and they'll have feathers and furs and everything to trade, only they'll bring it all to us. Pa said there'll be roads soon. So folks'll be able to come with horses and mules to stock up on supplies. We won't have to go to them."

"All we'll have to do is hang out the red trading flag and put up our sign. Think about it, Ma," begged Serena.

"Dowell's Emporium," shouted Newtie. "Come back to life and twice as lively!"

"Confuse and confound!" Ma sputtered. "You're goin' too fast for me. Let me think!"

They watched anxiously as she wrinkled her forehead in thought, then heaved sighs of relief as a broad smile finally spread over Ma's face. It was going to be all right.

"Hooray for our store!" yelled Luke.

"And our farm," added Newtie. They grabbed Serena's hands and pranced her around, leaping and hollering.

"Stop," Ma ordered. "The raft'll break apart. The pigs'll go right in the water." But she was laughing too. "We'll give it a try, anyway. Two stars to follow! And twice as much work, you know. We'll all have to work at followin' both stars, and don't you forget it. Serena, you're a pure wonderment." She added quickly, "Now hush your noise. The one that rouses Sweet Harmony has got to rock her to sleep again. Buildin' a farm is easier than that."

That quieted them. They pulled the pigs another measure of weeds and then followed Ma back to the meadow to wait for Pa.

It was a long, long afternoon. Time after time they wandered to the edge of the woods, hoping to hear Pa coming. But there was nothing to hear but the breeze rustling in the trees and the gentle cooing of wood pigeons.

Luke wanted to hunt for a spring, but Ma vetoed that. "No wanderin' off, now. Time enough to hunt for spring water when we find out for sure if we're to stay here. Meantime, fetch me another bucket of river water. We'll let the mud settle out of it for tomorrow's cookin'."

Serena and Newtie were glad of something to do, and when they came back with the water they were able to report that another boatload of settlers had gone by.

"See, Ma? Once we get settled, we'll have customers aplenty."

Ma nodded. "Seems likely. Now keep stirrin' these beans, keep 'em boilin'. The storm soaked them up so's they should cook fast. I'll make a batch of johnnycake to go with 'em. We'll have us a little feast to celebrate, soon's your pa shows his face. Hark, do you hear him?"

It wasn't Pa, just a squirrel thrashing through the treetops. The sun dropped down behind the woods and the blue shadows stretched all across the meadow.

"Build up the fire, boys. We'll have us a bonfire to light him home. And Serena, shorten Lilybelle's tether. Bring her in close. We — we wouldn't want her to miss the party."

Serena knew better than that. Night was coming on and they were in strange country. Luke quietly loaded the gun and laid it nearby.

"I might get a shot at a rabbit. Mmm, rabbit stew for breakfast." They all understood what the gun was for, even though no one said it.

Even Sweet Harmony was subdued for a change and sat quietly on Ma's lap, humming to her cornhusk doll.

Where was Pa, anyway? Had something happened to him? Serena pushed the thought out of her head as fast as it came, but the fear shoved back in again as the shadows grew deeper.

Pa *had* to come back safe. They needed Pa, all of them did. They needed his singing and laughing, they needed his knack of turning disaster into a joke. They needed Ma's horse sense and mother-wit too, to make it balance out. They make a good pair, Serena thought, and I'm a mishmash of the two of them, with all the good and the bad mixed up together.

She reached out for Ma's hand and gave it a good squeeze. "He'll be here soon, Ma. You wait and see."

Ma smiled at her. "You're a comfort to me, Serena, you surely are. You're growin' into your name."

Not really, Serena thought, but I'm willing to try.

Then the strained quiet was broken by a far-off shout. "Hello, Lucinda! Hello, Dowells!"

"Holler, all of you! Let him know where we are!"

When Pa trotted out of the woods he was met in grand noisy style.

"Wait till I tell you," he roared, hugging everyone all around. "Just you wait! Good news, Lucinda! Great news!"

"We're to stay here, Henry?" Ma's face was shining in the bright firelight, all the worry of the last hour gone now.

"No, we'll be movin' on."

"Oh." Her voice went flat with disappointment. "Someone else has got it staked out, then."

"Nope. Here, let's start eatin' while I tell it. I could eat a horse, saddle and bridle and all. I was a mite turned around back in the woods. Lost my direction when the sun went down. Then that cookin' smell drifted through the woods and brought me home a-runnin'."

Ma dished out the plates and they sat down, almost too excited to eat, while Pa told his story.

"Nope, no sign that this place is claimed. No sign that

I could find. But just beyond, no more'n a couple of miles, I stumbled on a site that'll make your eyes bug out. It's all you've been huntin' for, Lucinda, and more. There's a fast-runnin' little stream on the place, tumbles right down to the river, and if Luke is half as clever as we think he is he'll be able to rig up a mill wheel and harness that stream. We'll grow our own grain and grind it too. We can face the cabin to the east, Lucinda, so you'll get the morning light."

Ma clasped her hands. "I do enjoy the morning sun, Henry. Makes a house warmer and brighter. And Henry, let us tell you — "

He rushed on, eager to tell all the good things he had planned. "The land is high, and it slopes down nice and pleasant to the river. Someday we can have a landin' there, and maybe a boat for fishin'. And — "

Newtie couldn't wait any longer. "Pa! Pa, listen, there's something we have to tell *you* — "

Luke said quickly, "Let Serena tell. She's the one who thought it up. Go ahead, Serena."

She didn't know how to break the news. "Is — is there a good place there for a store?"

"A store?" Pa stared at her. "I'll have another piece of that cornbread, Lucinda. What store?"

"Dowell's Emporium, that's what! We're going to follow both stars, Pa, both of them. Oh, Pa, say you're pleased!"

It took a while to get it all straight, what with everyone talking at once, but when the plan was clear Pa was the most pleased man they had ever seen.

[143]

"Yippee!" he yelled. "I'm a red-hot snappin' turtle! I'm a ring-tailed roarer! I'm a wild-eyed hoppin' alligator of a storekeeper! Yippee!"

"You forgot the barbed-wire tail." Ma laughed.

"I'm pure grateful," he said when his wild capering dance was over. "It'll work out, Lucinda. We'll make it work, and I thank you from the bottom of my heart."

"Thank Serena," said Ma. "She was the one who saw it could be done. We just followed along after she pointed it out."

Pa gave Serena a bear hug. His beaming face was all the thanks she needed.

"The farm comes first," he planned. "We'll patch the raft tomorrow and float our stuff downriver. Then we'll build the cabin fast as we can, and dig us up a garden patch. And when the seeds are all in I'll go back upriver to Pittsburgh for a load of new store goods. I can get a ride both ways, no problem there. I'll take one of you along to help me, Luke or Newtie — "

"Or Serena," said Luke.

"We'll take turns," said Newtie. "There'll be plenty of trips, and we can take turns."

Serena's cup of happiness was running over. Two stars to follow, and the boys were counting her in. It was almost too much. But all she could think of to say was, "Please, may I have another helping of beans?"